Bogus to Bubbly

READ THE WHOLE SERIES:

Uglies
Pretties
Specials
Extras

Bogus to Bubbly

AN INSIDER'S GUIDE TO THE WORLD OF UGLIES

SCOTT WESTERFELD

SIMON PULSE
New York London Toronto Sydney

SIMON PULSE
An imprint of Simon & Schuster Children's Publishing Division
1230 Avenue of the Americas, New York, NY 10020
Text copyright © 2008 by Scott Westerfeld
Illustrations copyright © 2008 by Craig Phillips
All rights reserved, including the right of reproduction in whole
or in part in any form.
SIMON PULSE and colophon are registered trademarks of
Simon & Schuster, Inc.
Designed by Jane Archer
Manufactured in the United States of America
First Simon Pulse edition October 2008
10 9 8 7 6 5 4 3 2 1
Library of Congress Control Number 2008928643
ISBN-13: 978-1-4169-7436-9
ISBN-10: 1-4169-7436-9

This book is dedicated to the vibrant, brilliant, and always alert commenters at scottwesterfeld.com/blog, particularly those who helped create it by responding to my January 12, January 19, and March 5, 2008, posts:

Netta-la, Serafina Zane, Jenny, Razz, Lizi, Rosie-wa, ImInLoveWithJonathan!, sasheee-wa, Kenina-chan, max m, Amelia-wa, Shausto-la, Shloopy, Lena-la, Ally, Laura-la, Emily, Lickinley, Bran-la, Hoba-wa, Alisha-la, Robin-wa, Fallen, lotti-wa, courtney-wa, Em G, letticia, casey-wa, Bre-la, Mary Elizabeth S., Amber, Rainy, Danielle-wa, Tally & Zane, Mioki-la, laine-wa, Sarah, oOBubblesOo, Lae, SoPhIe-La, Tommy, Amy~la, Nicky-wa, Lizzy-wa, Allie, Liset, crim, Morganne-la, SpecialCircumstances, Emma-wa, Soleta, Kate-la, tali-wa, tesa-wa, Addie-wa, peyton-la, Brittany, The Risen Lilith, Savvy-la loves David, Marie, Kataqu, Amanda-wa, Little Willow, bella-wa, Michelle, JD, twisted words, Jen, Amber-la, SAM-la, Katie, jme-la, Jess, Carly, llamaturtle1717, jossy, Melanie, Shelli-wa, Lee-la, KawaiiOkashi, Meg, Jacki-la, Dylan, Bellac, Ann~la, SaRah, Hiro-Sensei, tally+david=love, Amy, Kay-wa, Use your imagination!, Katya, Sabrina, SHERIN, katela, Amethyst, Aubrey, Zane, *BRI*, Miles-wa, Madisonian, Jackie, Addyy, Vanessa, Taryn-la, Audrey-sensei, Hannah-la, lee, vivis, Bev-la, rAcHeL-wA, Mira-la, Bo Bo-la, molly-wa, monika, Tia, Caitlinn-wa, Jess-la, Cassie, Kara-la, Brianna-la, Grace-la, Julie-wa, Maddie-wa, Jonny, Lolita-wa, shayla, DavidandZaneLuver, Bubblebrained4EVER, tilly-la, Gina-la, Springdale, Tasha-wa,

Tatiana-la, Paige-la, Haley~Hyperness is BUBBLY!, Ju-Ju, alison, jordan, Jance-wa, Lea-wa!, Brynn-la, maya, Reagan, jaysa, SoccerChick, alex, dr. clarrissa, Sara-Chan, saudi-la, Tori-wa, Isabelle, Samantha-la, Nikki, Miranda, Chelle, Ali-wa, Juli-chan, sara-senei, peri-wa, Larissa, Holly-wa, mic, meghan-la, we pretties, Lydia, CJ, Eri-la, Rex-la, Michelle-la, ana-chan, Shey-la, risa-la, brooke, Momo, Bethany, Taylor-wa, chelsea, Ellie-wa, A, Andrea-La, bri-la, Gabrielle, sera zane, Bibliophone117, Susan-la, Risa, Allie, dragonfly, lucia, Haley Rae, kitty-la, Kadie-wa, Tatiana, ceenindee, katela, kim, Coloriifiiic, Haley-la, Alwyn, ILOVEDAVIDANDTALLY!, Becca-la, Shay-la, Cameo, Dessometrics, katrina, Heather R., Steph-la loves Edward, tally&david2gether4evr, max1milian, Clarissa-wa, Kailyn-la, Cat-kha, Renee-wa, elle, amanda perz, Miki !, Miss Independent, Macy-Wa, Prue-la, Lanie-wa-la-sensei, Shan-la, Erin-la, Sarah-Chan, Dia-la, Brooke-la, Framers, Leksey, Samara-la, Tee-la, IREALLYLOVEDAVID, Ghia, Laura Moncur, Eddie, Kristina-la, Maria-la, Amay-la, carri-la, Talulia-wa, nina-wa, Becki-la, court-la, Sam-la, krstn, Abby-wa, intensegreeneyes, ray-la, Sandra-la, bla, Irene-la, Addie-la, Riderchilde-wa, ZIE-sensei, Liv-wa, tara bear-la, Mikala-wa, Uglies Fan 101, katy-wa, Reese, Kailyx, Jordan :)1, alimionie, Hope-Potato, zoe-la, Rachael-wa, kirsten-chan, shaylee, colleen, meg-la, Topaz, Kenzie, laura-wa, Helena-Anne, Whitney-la, Karen-la, Britty-la, raz-la, no one, Sailor-wa, Ann-la, Crea-wa, Geslepen, Karissa, angee-sensei, Berii La, Kirsten, Ellie-la, Christy-la, sandy-wa, Evan-la, joanna-la, backbrry, Jessica, and capt. cockatiel.

It wouldn't have been as much fun without you!

CONTENTS

*Nature . . . didn't need an operation
to be beautiful. It just was.*

—UGLIES

THE BIG IDEA

Where did you get the idea for that nose?

—FRIZZ

One of the most common questions writers are asked is, "Where do you get your ideas?" But the sad truth is, we don't know. Ideas can come al any time and from any direction: in the shower, waiting for an elevator, or while bouncing across Wikipedia pages.

Even if we don't know for sure how books come into our heads, we still like making up answers for this dreaded question, and eventually these stories stick. So if you've ever seen me speaking in public, you've probably already heard this tale, pretty much word for word.

But just because I always tell it the same way, doesn't make it true. . . .

HOW I GOT THE IDEA FOR *UGLIES*

Many years ago one of my New York friends got a job in Los Angeles. We were all nervous for him. *He* was nervous for him, because Los Angelinos can be weird. For one thing, they have this crazy theory that LA is the center of the universe. This, of course, is offensive to us New Yorkers, given that New York City really *is* the center of the universe.

I mean, all they've got is beaches and movie stars, right? Whereas we have muggers, the subway, and tortured intellectuals. There's really no competition.

After my friend moved to LA, he would write us long, funny e-mails about his culture shock. My favorite described a visit to a Los Angeles dentist. At first it all seemed pretty normal: He sat in a chair, he rinsed and spat, the dentist poked and prodded. But after her inspection of his teeth was over, the dentist sighed and said, "I'm sorry, but it looks like I need to see you in my office."

"Er, okay," said my friend, wondering if he had teeth cancer or something.

He followed her back to a wood-paneled office, plaques covering the walls, and they both sat down. She made a tent with her fingers, leaned across the desk, and looked at him carefully, as if considering how to break bad news to him. Finally she said, "I need to ask you a serious question. Where do you want your teeth to be in five years?"

My friend stared at her. It wasn't exactly what he'd been expecting.

"Um, in my mouth?" he ventured.

"Yes, very amusing," she said. "But seriously, I think we need to talk about a five-year plan for your teeth."

My friend continued to stare, completely flummoxed. He didn't know anyone with a five-year plan for their teeth. Was this some sort of LA practical joke?

This confusion lasted for a few minutes, until finally the dentist explained using a simple diagram. Basically, at one end of the scale were my friend's teeth: normal, slightly coffee-stained New Yorker teeth. And at the other end, in the vanishing distance, were . . . Tom Cruise's teeth.

You know: Tom Cruise has these superwhite, supereven glowing teeth that shine like a spotlight when he smiles. So the dentist was asking: Over the next five years, how much pain did he want to endure and how much money did my friend want to spend on his journey toward Tom Cruise–like teeth?

My friend answered, "Um, I'll get back to you on that."

He left the dentist's office and walked around—this

was one of the few parts of LA with sidewalks and actual pedestrians—and as he stared at people, my friend kept wondering: *Who else has a five-year plan?*

Then he noticed a woman who might have had a five-year plan; she was about 25 percent of the way to Tom Cruise. And a man whose teeth were even whiter and straighter—like, 50 percent. And finally he saw a woman whose teeth shone like floodlights—even in the middle of the day—she *had gone out the other side* of Tom Cruise!

Did she have a *ten-year* plan?

All of us back in New York thought this e-mail was hilarious. Those crazy Los Angelinos and their teeth! But the story also got me thinking: What would the world be like if *everyone* had a five-year plan? Not just for their teeth but for their hair and skin and eyes? What if going to the doctor wasn't about your health at all, but about how you wanted to look?

What if cosmetic surgery was so common that you *had* to get it, or you'd be an outcast?

With this notion in my head, I started researching plastic surgery, the science of beauty, and a million other things I needed to know to create a believable future: magnetic levitation, nanotechnology, and, of course, brainwashing (because that's an important part of what's going on here). Slowly, Tally's world started to fall into place, and all the betrayals, victories, and defeats that she and her friends live through.

But it's still a bit odd to think that it all began with a trip to the dentist.

What follows are my notes on the process: the decisions about the characters, the settings, and the science and technology behind the world of *Uglies*. I've also included a few documents that you'd be able to read if you could somehow visit that world: a history book, a hoverboard manual, and a few maps.

I hope you enjoy them.

HOVERBOARD MANUAL

Never bored on a hoverboard.

—SHAY

The most common wish I hear from *Uglies* fans is that someone would get busy inventing a hoverboard. This desire even beats a non-bubblehead version of the operation. Ask yourself this: Would you trade a pretty face for the ability to fly? I certainly would.

Almost all my books have some kind of flying, climbing, or falling in them. That's partly because I've always had flying dreams, and I have this thing about heights. In college I used to climb buildings for fun, as a way of exploring the campus and hacking the physical world. (But please don't try this at home—or at school.)

Being up in the air is a dramatic way for characters to see their world from a new perspective—literally, I suppose. As Zane says in *Pretties*, "Nothing like heights to keep you bubbly." Even in our world, where flying is commonplace and amazingly boring, it still is a part of our dreams, and falling is a mainstay of our nightmares.

Of course, in Tally's world hoverboards weren't just for fun. This was the machine that freed tricky uglies from the boundaries of their cities, after all, allowing them to travel through the wild to the Rusty Ruins and the Smoke. It was only after exploring the world that Tally and Shay realized how many things needed changing. A few magnetic lifters meant the difference between joining the revolution and being stuck in their dorm rooms.

So what would it be like to requisition your own hoverboard? Luckily, the historians of the Awesome Librarians clique discovered this vintage user's manual in the memory stick of an old public wallscreen. As you read it, just imagine you're standing on your first hoverboard, ready to test your tricks against dorm monitors, safety trackers, and the edges of the grid.

CONGRATULATIONS on your requisition of a Series 9 Hoverboard!

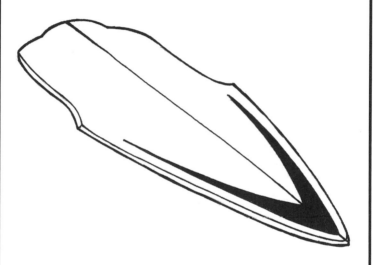

You have countless hours of flying ahead of you, but it's important to read these safety and control tips *before* jumping on board. That's why your hoverboard has been shipped with uncharged lifters. Place it near a public energy point, and it will be ready to go in only two hours! **Please read the following carefully. The life you save may be your own.**

THE HISTORY OF HOVERING

Flying is so easy these days that we sometimes forget what a complex machine a hoverboard is. Simplicity of use is the result of high technology and two centuries of careful testing and design. Ever since the Rusty Crash made it clear that internal combustion was a planet-wrecking idea, scientists realized that an efficient, electricity-based form of travel was something the world couldn't survive without.

These days, magnetic levitation has become the primary means of transportation. This leaves our cities much more space for trees, soccer fields, and pleasure gardens, because we don't have to cover everything with paved roads like the Rusties did. Our "roads" are invisible because they're buried under the ground!

THE GRID

Using the remains of the Rusty Ruins around us, your city government has built a grid, a lattice of ferrous metal buried a few meters below the ground. (Ferrous metals have iron in them, which means they can interact with magnetic forces.) This grid gives your hoverboard something to push against. So the higher you fly, and the farther your board's lifting magnets are from the grid, the weaker they become. How high you can fly depends on your weight and how much charge remains in your board.

WARNING: Never attempt to use your hoverboard outside city limits! Dangers include sudden speed reduction, loss of control, and contact with the ground.

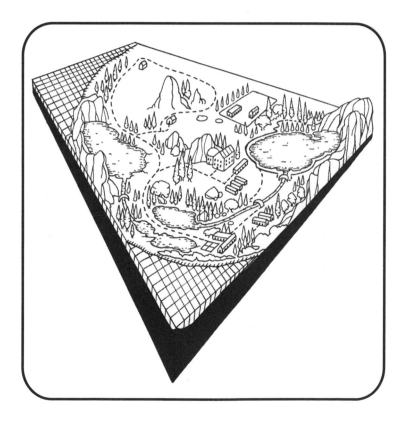

YOUR BOARD

Your Series 9 Hoverboard incorporates three main systems:

❶ Electromagnetic lifters powerful enough to levitate the board's weight and yours, and to propel you forward at speeds of up to eighty kilometers per hour. Of all your hoverboard's components, the lifters use most of the energy. Flying at high speeds or high altitudes and carrying extra weight can all greatly reduce the time between charges.

NOTE: Lifters are mostly solid metal and therefore extremely heavy. But, as you will discover when carrying your board, the lifters function in "background mode," reducing the board's weight to only a few kilograms. If your board feels unusually heavy, chances are it needs to be recharged.

❷ A guidance-and-control system that makes the board do what you want. The control system reacts to your gestures, shifts in weight, and even sounds, like snapped fingers and verbal commands. Boards also react to the position of your hands (see "Crash Bracelets") and your center of gravity (see "Belly Sensor"). As you ride your board more and more, its control system will learn your particular way of flying, until it seems to be almost reading your thoughts!

> **NOTE:** To lock your board's control system so that only you can use it, set the identity check to INTERFACE RING or EYESCAN. Series 9 boards can also be placed in "free mode," where anyone can use them.

❸ A safety system to protect riders from collisions and from themselves. Series 9 boards are always in touch with your city interface, so that the boards know where they are. City regulations may require you to stay away from restricted and congested areas. Some boards are shipped preprogrammed to keep away from the edge of the city grid, where they can fall out of the sky. Depending on the city you live in, your board's safety system may also restrict you to safe speeds.

> **NOTE:** Riders who trick their hoverboards by removing official tracking devices and safety governors risk serious injury and even death!

ACCIDENTS

Even the most experienced hoverboard riders have accidents. As a new rider, you will find yourself falling off your board more than once in the first few days. But don't worry, just read the following sections carefully, and don't forget to practice, practice, practice!

CRASH BRACELETS

A pair of crash bracelets is your most important piece of hoverboard safety equipment. Each bracelet contains its own magnetic lifter that is capable of arresting a fall of up to a hundred meters. Of course, this doesn't mean you *want* to fall off your hoverboard. Being stopped by your wrists at high speeds can result in injuries, including broken bones, muscle damage, and dislocated shoulders. Please see an autodoc after all hoverboard falls.

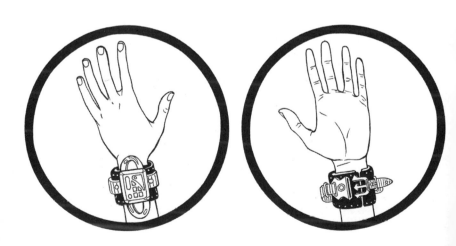

NOTE: The lifters in your crash bracelets have their own batteries and must be kept charged. If your crash bracelets are low on energy, your hoverboard's safety system will warn you before you take off.

NOTE: Crash bracelets are designed to work over a city grid. Using your hoverboard over wild sources of metal (such as streambeds) may result in crash bracelets not working as intended. *Stay inside city limits!*

Crash bracelets have three other important functions:

1 If you fall off, your board will stop and drift back to find you, using the bracelets as a tracking beacon.

2 Your Series 9 board constantly tracks the position of your bracelets as you ride. This helps its guidance-and-control system know how you are standing on the board, so it can try to anticipate your next move.

3 If your board is out of sight, you can call it by twisting the CALL ring on your crash bracelets. It will fly toward you from anywhere in your city at a safe, even speed.

CONTROLLING YOUR BOARD

Hoverboards are designed to make riders feel as though they are gliding across an invisible surface. If you think about it that way, most movements have logical results. For example:

Leaning right or left turns the board in that direction.

Leaning forward increases speed.

Leaning backward, and tipping the front of the board up, slows the board down.

RIDING TIPS

- Always wear grippy shoes when hoverboarding! (Requisition separately.)

- Keep your feet apart for better balance.

- Extend your arms, both for balance and to help your board anticipate your motions.

- Don't be afraid to exaggerate your movements when riding a new hoverboard. Then, as the board learns your specific style, you can gradually make your motions more subtle.

PERSONAL COMMANDS

Boards can also be programmed to react to sounds, words, and gestures. The only limit is your imagination. (See "Programming Techniques" in our advanced manual.) Your board comes preprogrammed with the following simple commands:

Snapping your fingers causes your hoverboard to rise.

Pointing both thumbs down causes your board to lose altitude.

Crossing your wrists over your chest signals an emergency to the city interface.

The following items are available for requisition separately:

BELLY SENSOR

If you normally wear a belly ring, you may wish to consider clipping on a belly sensor while you ride. Your board's guidance-and-control system will track the exact position of your belly sensor, which tells it where your center of gravity is at any moment. Combined with other data—the shifting of your weight on the board, the position of your crash bracelets, and your verbal commands—your center of gravity helps the board sense how you are standing and where you want to go next.

Center of Gravity

Hand Position

Foot Position

LONG-RANGE HOVERBOARD

Once you have mastered riding inside city limits, you may want to take a hoverboard on your next camping trip. But boards designed for the city are very dangerous when used off the grid. Consider requisitioning a long-range hoverboard with the following features:

Extra-strength lifters to use natural sources of metal to push against, such as those found in streams and rivers.

Extendable solar panels to recharge without city power points.

Metal-detector lights to continuously inform the rider of the amount of ferrous metal in the terrain.

MAPS

Geography is very important in the Uglies series. Take Tally's city, where the neighborhoods are laid out to reflect the culture's ideology. Uglies and pretties are divided not just by culture and tradition, but by the river and the greenbelt. Everyone knows his or her place!

Outside this ordered existence is the wild, a messy place that shows the scars of history. It's dotted with leftovers of the Crash: ruins, ecological disasters, and warring pre-Rusty reservations. And yet in their journeys across the wild, Tally and her friends also run into hopeful symbols of the future, such as Diego and the Smoke.

So this guide wouldn't be complete

without a few maps. Here are "the city" (that's right, I never gave it a name) and some of the North American continent (partly flooded by global warming, you'll notice). I hope they help to orient you in Tally's world.

TALLY'S CITY

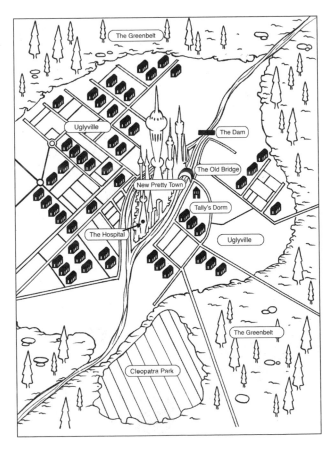

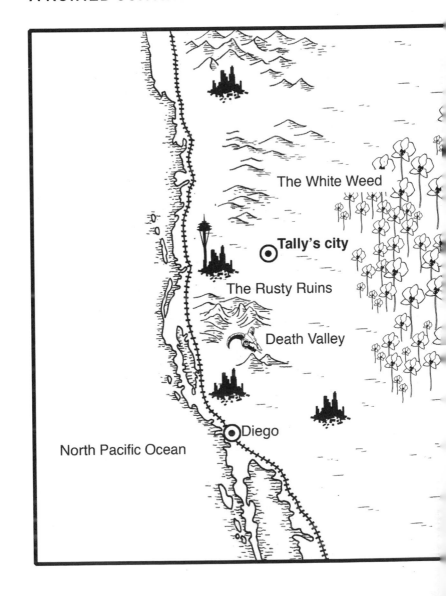

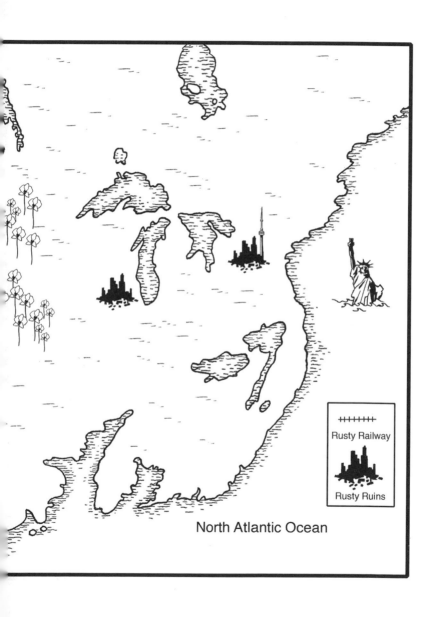

North Atlantic Ocean

+++++++
Rusty Railway

Rusty Ruins

THE HISTORY OF TALLY'S WORLD

A question I'm often asked is: "Are *we* the Rusties?"

The short answer is: "Yes!" But, of course, what I really mean is that we *could* be the Rusties. We don't have to wind up with a future like Tally's. We have a choice. That's why history is written *after* it happens, not before—because no one knows how things will turn out.

But if we do manage to take the same path as the Rusties in Tally's world, here's how all the history books three hundred years from now will start, by explaining how the people of today messed *everything* up. . . .

HISTORY #1:
THE RUSTY CRASH

What if there had been millions of Smokies? Billions of them, soon enough? Outside of our self-contained cities, humanity is a disease, a cancer on the body of the world.

—DR. CABLE

The Rusties were strange in a lot of ways, but perhaps the hardest thing to comprehend is how many there were: billions.

Yes, that's *billions* with a *b*!

That made them hard to count, so nobody knows exactly how many Rusties were alive during the Crash. But at some point before the end, Earth's population certainly reached 10 billion. That's about two hundred people for every square mile of land, which didn't leave a lot of room for prairies, tundra, deserts, or rain forests. More than half of Earth's land surface was taken over by human beings and the network of farms, mines, oil fields, and factories that supported them.

But it wasn't just the Rusties' numbers that were planet-wrecking, it was their appetites. They burned so much energy that at night their city lights could be seen from space. (No, we're not kidding.) And they loved to buy stuff—cars, electronics, unrecyclable clothes. In wealthy countries, the average Rusty produced two kilograms of garbage every single day. Multiply that amount by a few billion, and you get the picture.

To manufacture all this stuff, the Rusties gouged the earth and poisoned the sky. Their hunger wreaked havoc in the climate and in the codes of life itself. Under this constant assault, the wild began to die. At the Rusties' height, a hundred species became extinct every day.

They did a pretty good job on themselves too. Their political leaders were always looking for ways to kill one another, and their economic systems were built on poverty and debt. And so finally, one day, they got *too* good at destroying themselves.

No one knows who created the oil bug. Maybe it was a well-meaning Rusty scientist trying to solve the problem of oil spills. Or maybe it was a terrorist trying to bring down the established order. It may even have been a natural product of evolution, life itself striking back.

But however the oil bug appeared, there's no

denying that these tiny bacteria changed the world. Like mold consuming bread, they raced through any oil they came in contact with, changing its chemical structure. Overnight the gas in a Rusty car would become unstable, exploding on contact with the air. Suddenly every car was a bomb, every oil field a firestorm.

And as the oil burned, it carried the spores of the bug into the air. Soon the oil bug had spread across the entire world.

So why didn't people just change their ways when the bug was first discovered? Why did so many of them have to die?

Because the Rusties were hugely dependent on oil. They used 100 million barrels every day—to make plastic, to fertilize crops, to build roads, and to generate electricity. Even their clothing was made from oil-based products, along with their perfume, lipstick, nail polish . . . you name it.

With their cars aflame, they had no way to escape their giant cities. To make things worse, the planet was too broken to help the survivors—the rivers were dirty, the land wouldn't grow food. And, being Rusties, the people fought over everything that was left, compounding starvation with bloodshed. In that first decade, 98 percent of humanity died.

Of course, a few people survived. . . .

THE RISE OF THE CITIES AND THE PRETTY COMMITTEE

Or maybe when they do the operation—when they grind and stretch your bones to the right shape, peel off your face and rub all your skin away, and stick in plastic cheekbones so you look like everybody else— maybe after going through all that you just aren't very interesting anymore.

—SHAY

After the Rusty Crash were long years of hardship and warfare. None of the old nation states survived. Even cities and towns fell to pieces, dependent as they were on a system that had failed. But here and there, small groups of people managed to stick together and survive. They were a mixed bunch, and most were outside the mainstream.

Some were people who'd already rejected the Rusty system and had lived in the wilderness for a long time, more or less expecting civilization to fail. Some were villagers in the rain forests or deserts, who'd never been a part of the world that was falling apart. Some were scientists whose technical skills helped them navigate the challenges of the Crash, or remainders of the Rusties' vast armies, who were organized and better equipped to survive.

At first these groups were widely separated. The Crash had carved the world into pieces, centered around a few livable areas, with dead zones in between. Bioengineered species had swept across the ruined farms, making huge spaces uninhabitable. Even with the Rusties' factories and strip mines fallen silent, the wild was slow to recover. Too much damage had been done.

So when civilization did arise again, it was in small cities in a few safe areas, with vast spaces between them. These cities were also separated by differences in culture and background, some cities highly technical, some rustic, almost pre-Rusty. Some survivors blamed mysterious enemies or vengeful gods for the Crash, and some put the blame on Rusty civilization itself. Many of the cities, ironically, were settled just outside the Rusty Ruins.

But as they began to reach out across the wild and make contact with one another, the survivors discovered that they all shared a common conviction: The planet must not be wrecked again.

Gradually the cities established limited contact and began to trade and share technology. With oil gone they focused on renewable resources: solar and wind power. Superconductors made hover technology possible but limited travel to within cities, where magnetic grids could be constructed. No one was anxious to rebuild the highway systems of the Rusties.

Overall, it was a time of peace and cooperation. Earth's population was so small that there was little competition for territory. And after everything that had happened during the Crash, war just didn't seem like a great idea.

But there were still conflicts, because people still had different faiths and cultures, and still viewed one another with suspicion. Some people worried that one day the cities would grow strong enough to fight one another. And no one knew if old Rusty weapons still existed, waiting for someone to stumble upon them and use them again. Maybe next time the planet wouldn't recover.

So, about a century after the Crash, a group of scientists from every city convened to study the problem of human conflict. They studied the few pre-Rusty tribes outside the cities, who still fought one another in endless, bloody feuds. They plumbed old Rusty psychology texts, trying to find a means of eliminating war forever.

Then one day a researcher rediscovered an old theory called the "halo effect." Rusty science had shown that beautiful people were treated better than their peers, got into less trouble, and were more happy and successful. Perhaps if *everyone* were beautiful, the world would be a better and more peaceful place.

Over many years a surgical procedure was developed to turn young people into so-called pretties. Their faces would call on the basic evolutionary instincts of cooperation and courtship in everyone who looked at them. Cultural differences, personal hatred—nothing could stand against the power of a pretty face.

Of course, these first "pretties" weren't nearly as beautiful as pretties of later generations. But they were the prototype that started generations of experimentation and development, ushering in the beginning of the Prettytime, an era of peace and stability.

Of course, this was only the official story.

What scientists really discovered was that pretties

did fight with one another. No matter how beautiful they were, human beings still competed, still rebelled, and still sometimes hated one another. Maybe things were a litlle easier among the pretties, but something else had to be done if war were to be prevented forever.

Something far more drastic.

Fortunately for those in charge, everyone was dying to have the pretty surgery—who wouldn't want to be gorgeous, after all? If another answer could be found in the operating tank, maybe humanity could still be saved from itself.

That answer was, of course, bubblehead surgery.

With small alterations to several areas of the brain, a new kind of pretty could be created: compliant, unaggressive, and happy, the perfect combination of sweet-tempered and just a bit lazy. Impossible to make into soldiers, bubbleheads could never go to war. Incapable of dealing with more than one child every few decades, they certainly wouldn't re-create Rusty overpopulation anytime soon. And they were unlikely to ever want to change the system that had made them so beautiful and so happy. Finally humanity could be kept in an idyllic state forever—the end of hardship and conflict had been reached at last.

Of course, the Pretty Committee kept this new aspect of the pretty surgery secret. Nobody volunteers to have brain damage.

But the committee needed *some* people to be without the bubblehead effect. They had to sacrifice their own innocence and happiness to stay watchful, to govern and to guard against danger in a world of bubbly happiness. Which meant that while the vast majority of the human race was happily pretty-minded, a few people could still see cold, cruel reality, even if they were beautiful on the outside.

And gradually these non-bubbleheads started to see themselves as . . . special.

HISTORY #3:

SPECIAL CIRCUMSTANCES AND THE SMOKE

We don't want to hurt you, but we will if we have to.
—SPECIAL CIRCUMSTANCES ARREST SCRIPT

No one can say for sure who was the first Special.

It's a bit like evolution: You can't pick the first bird out from the feathered dinosaurs, or the first human being from the chimpanzees. But gradually, those people who kept apart from the rest of bubbleheaded humanity began to make themselves "better."

Some were police officers and firefighters, and after all, they needed to be stronger and faster than normal humans. Others were scientists who had to make cold and rational decisions to protect humanity from itself. Some were the last line of defense against troublemakers and runaways, a job that required a cruel beauty that commanded instant respect.

But they didn't become inhuman all at once. Each generation improved the next, growing stronger, colder, and more cruel-looking. Some of these people began to call themselves Special Circumstances, because they handled all the messy, unpredictable things that pretties weren't capable of facing. And after decades of being stronger, faster, and smarter than everyone else, the people in Special Circumstances really were different from the rest of humanity. But they didn't see themselves as freaks, they saw themselves as *special*.

So the rules no longer applied to them.

It was in Tally Youngblood's city that this separation was the most extreme. There, the Specials hid themselves from public view, becoming a secret government that most people knew about only through rumors. They pursued runaways, guarded the city's borders, and kept a watchful eye on humanity as a whole, making sure it would never wreck the planet again.

And they might have stayed in charge forever, if not for two doctors named Maddy and Az.

Like all doctors, Maddy and Az had been turned pretty, but were later cured of bubbleheadedness. They didn't realize this, of course. Only people in Special Circumstances knew the secret of the operation, so Maddy and Az just thought that they were smarter and more serious than most people.

But as they worked—Az as a surgeon and Maddy on the Global Pretty Committee—they began to notice that most pretties had something odd in their brains: small lesions, minor brain damage. Only a few pretties, those with jobs like firefighters, wardens, and doctors, didn't have these lesions. And even more strange was that uglies, children under sixteen who had not received the pretty operation, didn't have them at all.

They had discovered the awful secret that underlaid their society: Beauty wasn't enough to make people peaceful and compliant; you also had to alter their minds.

Maddy and Az's research was soon shut down by Special Circumstances, and the two decided to run away from the city, taking a handful of young uglies with them. Maddy, Az, and their uglies disappeared into the wild to found a community called "the Smoke." The Smokies borrowed technology from the cities, but also learned how to live in the wild again, like pre-Rusties (who had never lived in cities at all). The Smokies built houses with muscle power, raised animals, and even burned wood for heat and cooking. Managing to connect with some of the trickle of runaways who snuck out into the wild every year seeking adventure, they gradually grew in number. But for a long time the cities had no reason to suspect the Smoke existed.

Then everything changed—Maddy and Az had a son.

David was the first child raised in the Smoke, and he understood the wild instinctively, in a way that no city-born person could. But the cities—his parents' home that he had never seen—made him curious. As he grew older, he began to probe the edges of civilization and to explore the Rusty Ruins near the cities. There, he encountered some tricky uglies who were testing the boundaries of their own world.

David never failed to impress these city kids. He had a confidence they'd never seen before in an ugly or a pretty, and he understood mysteries of the wild that they never would grasp. The legend of David and of his secret home in the wilderness spread among uglies in several cities. Ugly cliques began to form with the express purpose of escaping to the Smoke.

David even found a few pretty allies, most from a southern city called Diego. Diego encouraged independent thinking. Traditionally, its teachers and librarians were cured of their lesions (like police officers were in other cities), so all Diegans were influenced by non-bubbleheads from birth. The city had no real Special Circumstances, but its Rangers, who were focused on preserving the environment, were spread out across the continent. These Rangers began to assist runaways who wanted to start a new life in the wild.

Soon, David was recruiting more runaways than the Smoke had ever seen. The community expanded, and rumors of its existence spread farther than ever before.

These events did not go unnoticed in other cities. Across the continent the agents of Special Circumstances wondered where their runaway uglies were disappearing to and began to watch more carefully. . . .

HISTORY #4:
CRIMS, CURES, AND DR. CABLE

The Smoke Lives.

—AN, DEX, AND SUSSY

Around this time in Tally's city, there was an ugly clique called "the Crims." Its six members were Croy, Ryde, Astrix, Ho, Shay, and Zane, their leader. These early Crims were typical tricky uglies, hoverboarding and sneaking into New Pretty Town, an area where the pretties lived within every city. The Crims had heard rumors of the Smoke and dreamed of living there one day. So when they at last encountered David in the Rusty Ruins near their city, they began to plan. The Crims chose the eve of Zane's sixteenth birthday to make their escape.

Four of them made it to the Smoke, but Zane and Shay were too afraid to leave everything they knew. Zane became pretty as scheduled and re-formed the Crims as a pretty clique, and Shay was alone in

Uglyville. She soon met Tally Youngblood, beginning a momentous and tumultuous friendship that would change the world forever.

What Shay didn't know was that she was being watched. After the Crims' escape, the local head of Special Circumstances had interrogated Zane before his pretty operation. This very determined Special, Dr. Cable, threatened to keep him ugly forever unless he told her everything he knew. She was obsessed with the possibility of humanity escaping the bonds of the pretty operation and threatening the planet again. Dr. Cable feared that the Smokies would reveal the truth about the Prettytime to the wider world, and made their capture her personal mission. Zane told her about David, the secret paths to the Rusty Ruins, and the existence of the Smoke. But he didn't know its location.

The Smokies had always been careful. They checked runaways for tracking devices and used coded clues instead of maps to guide them. These precautions made it unlikely that many outsiders would ever find the Smoke.

So when Shay disappeared to the Smoke a few nights before *her* sixteenth birthday, Dr. Cable realized that Shay's new friend, Tally, might be useful. Faced with the threat of remaining ugly forever, Tally was forced to follow Shay to the Smoke and betray the runaways.

At first the plan worked: Tally set off across the wild on her own, and reached the Smoke, following a set of clues left behind by Shay. She decided to join the Smokies' cause, but accidentally activated a tracking device. Special Circumstances arrived and captured almost all the Smokies. Only David and Tally remained free.

History, of course, shows that these two were more resourceful than Dr. Cable could have imagined. They traveled back across the wild to Tally's city and managed to free several Smokies (including Maddy) from Special Circumstances headquarters. These renegades formed the New Smoke, dedicated not merely to escaping the cities but to ending the rule of the pretty regime forever.

The New Smokies' most important accomplishment was the invention of a treatment known as "the cure." These nano-pills reversed the effects of the bubblehead operation, returning pretties to their normal intelligence and willpower. The first recipient of the cure was to be Tally Youngblood, who gave herself up to the authorities to become pretty so that she could serve as a test subject. But once again the Crims found themselves making history.

After Zane's operation he had restarted his old clique, gathering new pretties who had been tricky in their ugly life. The Crims were focused on staying "bubbly"—trying to recall their days as rebellious uglies. Without realizing it they were naturally fighting the effects of the bubblehead operation. Recaptured Smokies like Tachs and Tally joined the Crims, adding their knowledge of the wild to Zane's enthusiasm. So when the cure was smuggled to Tally, she shared the pills with Zane.

As the cure took hold of his mind, Zane planned a mass escape of the Crims. Dozens of them fled the city in one night. Tally, Zane, and several others were soon recaptured, but the other escapees gave the New Smokies a huge boost in number and in technical skills.

The New Smoke began to distribute the cure in several cities, including Tally's. Hundreds, then thousands, and finally tens of thousands of people gradually found their bubbleheadedness fading.

The world was waking up.

HISTORY #5:
THE DIEGO WAR

This city was never like ours. They didn't have the same barriers between pretties and uglies.

—FAUSTO

Nowhere were the effects of the New Smokies' cure more profound than in the city of Diego, where independent thinking had always been encouraged. In fact, Diego's government greeted the changes with enthusiasm, admitting the truth about the operation to their citizens. (Other cities continued to keep the secret, though rumors soon began to spread.) Diego announced a "New System," in which citizens could have their bubblehead surgery reversed.

In an unexpected side effect, repealing the Pretty Committee's guidelines caused an explosion in strange new surgeries. People used their bodies as canvases for self-expression, and the strict lines between uglies and pretties began to crumble.

More fatefully, the New System guaranteed that *anyone* could become a citizen of Diego for the purpose of being cured—even pretty runaways from other cities. Diego's Rangers coordinated with the New Smokies, setting up escape routes to help runaways reach sanctuary.

Of course, the Special Circumstances of other cities found events in Diego disturbing. As the cure spread, their own citizens were showing signs of the bubblehead operation wearing off. Pretties were questioning the social order and demanding more freedoms. How could the Specials guard the world if everything was out of order?

Something had to be done about the New System and all it represented. And Dr. Cable soon decided that she should be the one to do it. The stage for the Diego War was set. . . .

In another twist of history, it was Tally Youngblood who provided the reason for war.

After their mass escape, Tally, Shay, and several other recaptured Crims had fallen into Dr. Cable's hands. Using surgery and brainwashing techniques, she had made them into a new group of Specials called Cutters. These Cutters were violent and self-reliant, their bodies modified for military use and capable of living in the wild for long periods of ti... Dr. Cable's purpose for them was to track down the New Smokies, but these young, independent-minded Specials proved hard to control—and even dangerous. While arranging an illegal escape for Zane and his friends, Tally and Shay accidentally destroyed their city's military archive. Dr. Cable couldn't admit that her own Specials were so out of control, and blamed the attack on her current obsession: Diego.

Tally's city's government was already nervous—the cure was spreading, politics had become tumul-tuous, and more uglies were escaping every day. Even pretties were running away. The civilian authorities, believing that the New System had brought back the insanity of war, gave Dr. Cable temporary command of the entire city.

The only real battle of the war was an attack on Diego Town Hall, the city's center of administration and government. Dr. Cable's military drones swept into Diego in the middle of the night and destroyed the building. Although no one was inside Town Hall, seventeen patients in the adjacent hospital were killed (including, most famously, Zane).

The attack may have been a military success, but it was a political disaster for Dr. Cable. Other cities condemned the invasion, horrified that war had returned to plague humanity after more than two centuries of peace. And when Diego broadcast interviews with Shay and other cured members of the Cutters, the sight of sixteen-year-olds with military body modifications shocked the entire world.

With its town hall destroyed, Diego staggered through the next few weeks. But soon the value of the New System revealed itself: Cured people could function in an emergency far better than bubbleheads. The wardens, Rangers, and cured Cutters helped to organize the citizenry and keep Diego functioning.

Back in Tally's city, Dr. Cable was discovering how many of the citizens under her control had already been cured by smuggled pills. They began to question her leadership, and her grip on power slowly slipped. People even began to debate surgical "despecialization," a final end to Special Circumstances.

Dr. Cable was removed from power a few weeks after the attack on Diego. Specials across the continent were scheduled for despecialization, and the last military archives were destroyed. The cured Cutters in Diego were allowed to keep their physical powers thanks to their service in the war. But ultimately, the only true Special on the continent was Tally Youngblood, who disappeared into the wild just as the war was coming to an end.

As the cure took hold in more cities, the truth about the operation began to spread. Within another year the bubblehead procedure was no longer being performed on the continent.

But the forces unleashed as the Prettytime ended were harder to control than anyone (except maybe Tally) had predicted. As the cure spread, overturning two centuries of stability and peace, a new term came into use for the New System, the new inventions, and the strange new social orders coming into existence.

The "mind-rain" had begun to fall.

HISTORY #6:
THE MIND-RAIN AND THE EXTRAS

Freedom has a way of destroying things.

—TALLY YOUNGBLOOD

The mind-rain first took hold in the western half of the North American continent. And once Diego had rebuilt itself, the New Smokies set about to transform the rest of the world.

Teams of agents traveled first to South America and the eastern seaboard. In each city they recruited the tricky uglies they encountered on the edges of the wild. The cure was propagated through these young people and spread into every city like the tendrils of a vine.

Reinforced by new recruits as they went, the New Smokies soon moved on to Africa, Europe, Australia, and Asia. But as they traveled farther from home, they discovered something unexpected: Many cities had already "cured" themselves. Governments had seen the changes on the global feeds and didn't want to be left behind in an era of technological and social innovation. So they had elected to join in the mind-rain on their own.

Of course, a few cities were like Tally's, with local Special Circumstances ready to fight any change. But the New Smokies discovered that every society had its own Crims, discontents who were more than willing to subvert the social order. And for the most hard-to-crack places, the New Smokies called in the Cutters with their superhuman powers to impose the cure.

Nearer to home, other New Smokies worked with the few pre-Rusty tribes who had survived outside the cities. These people had been kept in a Stone Age state for research purposes, and many of them now wanted to be integrated into the rest of the world.

But as the mind-rain fell, what exactly was that world becoming?

For two centuries the bubblehead operation had suppressed human imagination and will. Technology, the arts, and culture had stagnated. But now *anyone*, not just official scientists, could use the vast resources of the city interfaces to study, to experiment, and to share their knowledge with the rest of humanity. Global creativity was about to explode.

A host of new technologies were invented in

the first years of the mind-rain: eyescreens, smart matter, and hoverball rigs, to name a few. People also set about reclaiming all that had been *lost* during the Prettytime: Ancient rituals, local customs, and old religions were rediscovered, along with all the family traditions that had been discouraged by keeping uglies and pretties separate.

A more sinister change occurred in the rules that the cities had lived by. For two centuries there had been no mining for metals, no burning of fossil fuels, and no clear-cutting of forests. But as the mind-rain fell, the old Rusty appetites emerged. The cities began to swell, encroaching upon the wild with new suburbs and factories.

The Expansion had begun.

Of course, Tally Youngblood had predicted all this. In her famous "Manifesto," she had declared herself and David to be the "New Special Circumstances," ready to protect the wild in any way necessary.

No one doubted her willingness to intervene, especially when, one year into the mind-rain, a mining operation near the city of Londinium was destroyed in a suspicious nano accident. As populations increased, so did the pressure for resources, and soon the cities turned to a new source. During the Prettytime, the Rusty Ruins had been carefully preserved as monuments to waste. But the Rusties' ancient structures were suddenly valuable: They were full of metal that could be recycled to make new buildings. Here was an easy way to keep expanding without tempting the wrath of New Special Circumstances.

But the metal from the ruins couldn't last forever, and then what would happen?

As the Expansion grew in strength, a secret and global clique called the Extraterrestrials (or Extras) was formed. Their leader, a man named Udzir, had determined that the only way to protect Earth from humanity was to move humanity *off the planet*.

The Extras began to develop technologies for orbital communities. They experimented with radical new operations, readying themselves to live in an environment of zero gravity. Not wanting to alarm the metal-dependent cities, they gathered materials in secret from Rusty Ruins across the globe. Megatons of metal were smuggled to a hidden base in Southeast Asia, and a fleet of spaceships was constructed to effect this "New Expansion."

When this secret base was discovered by Tally Youngblood with the help of a young story-kicker named Aya Fuse, a series of misunderstandings almost led to its destruction. But since that time, the Extras have worked in the open, recruiting new members every day for their grand scheme of living in near-Earth orbit.

The Extras' First Fleet has recently launched, and a dozen orbital habitats have been constructed. So far the New Expansion seems to be working—tens of thousands of people live in space, requiring only negligible supplies from the mother planet.

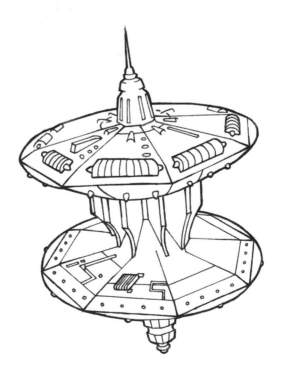

• • •

But space isn't for everyone—many of us don't want to replace our legs with an extra set of arms, for example. So, for those who choose to stay on Earth, the issue of how to pursue our dreams while preserving our planet remains. Perhaps some big idea like the New Expansion will emerge from the creative cauldron of the mind-rain, solving the problem of overextended resources once and for all.

Or maybe we'll simply learn to ask every time we want something: Is this shiny new toy worth carving up another fraction of the earth?

Because we don't want to fail that test too many times. Tally Youngblood is still out there watching to make sure we don't go too far.

LIFE PHASES IN THE PRETTYTIME

Once we turn, it's new pretty, middle pretty, late pretty. Then dead pretty.

—SHAY

Here's another document uncovered by the Awesome Librarians clique. Written in Aya Fuse's time, after the mind-rain, it explains how the world used to work: how littlies became uglies, then pretties, and finally crumblies.

Back in the Prettytime, the phases of life were carefully defined. Except for young children and their parents, people of different ages lived apart from one another. They obeyed different rules, entertained themselves in different ways, even spoke different languages.

This system wasn't an accident. It allowed the government to control each age group in its own way, by rewarding the behavior they wanted from that group. Most important, separating people who had undergone the bubblehead operation from those who hadn't made it easier to conceal its true purpose. Because new pretties lived apart from others, their parents and younger friends found it easy to believe that humans suddenly became brain-missing *as a natural result* of turning sixteen.

Of course, these phases of life have become less rigid since the mind-rain. To understand that world, you will have to cast your mind back to the time of uglies, pretties, and crumblies, when how old you were was *what* you were.

Littlies

From birth to age eleven, children lived with their middle-pretty parents in the suburbs. (Anyone who had children was, almost by definition, a middle pretty.) Littlies went to elementary school with other kids their age but maintained strong relationships with their parents. This was the only stage of life when traditional family ties were considered appropriate. In many cities, middle pretties were encouraged to have only one child every decade. This helped control the population and kept strong sibling bonds from forming.

NOTE: *In many cities the suburbs were separated from Uglyville by a swath of forest called "the greenbelt." This geographical boundary enforced the differences between ages—leaving your parents' home required crossing a symbolic "wild zone" of trees and parks. Littlies were discouraged from playing in the greenbelt, which was reserved as a place for uglies to act out their wild impulses.*

Uglies

At age twelve children left home to live in dorms in a part of town known as Uglyville. Away from their families for the first time, they went through systematic social programming. They were encouraged to insult one another with ugly nicknames like Slouch, Fatty, or Beady-Eyes. They wore only dorm uniforms, which were basic and unflattering.

This programming caused them to look forward to the day when they would turn sixteen and have the operation. With such a low self-image, it was uncommon for any ugly to question the need for an entirely new face and body.

Ugly dorms were heavily monitored by drones and other surveillance devices, but uglies often subverted the rules and machines that governed their lives. It is believed that in Tally's city, the government allowed, even encouraged, these tricks as a way of spotting personalities that might cause trouble later on. The rebellious uglies were monitored even after the operation, and those most resistant to bubbleheadedness were recruited for jobs that required aggressiveness and independent thinking. (See "Middle Pretties.")

NOTE: *In Tally Youngblood's city, Uglyville was separated from New Pretty Town by a wide river, which uglies were forbidden to cross without permission. This prevented them from keeping in touch with their older friends who had already had the operation, helping to hide the bubblehead effect.*

NEW PRETTIES

When uglies turned sixteen (or seventeen or later in some cities), they underwent surgery to become new pretties. The operation was, of course, many small operations: a full skin graft, cosmetic surge, body morphology change, and the replacement of teeth and other bones with stronger materials. Most important, and secret, was a form of brain surge developed early in the post-Crash era. This "bubble-head surge" made human beings much less aggressive and less inquisitive, overall less likely to question the social order.

Of course, human brains are very good at rewiring themselves after being damaged in this way (some more so than others). Thus, the effects of the bubblehead surge were more obvious in new pretties, who had recently had the operation. As a way of hiding this so-called bubblehead effect, new pretties were kept apart from people in other stages of life. In addition, new-pretty culture was full of mindless distractions: drinking, bungee jumping, hot-air ballooning, all organized around nightly fireworks displays and parties.

New pretties had huge clothing allowances by current standards, and new-pretty cliques demanded slavish devotion to fashion—those who didn't dress, talk, and act like everyone else were voted out of the cliques. In a place like New Pretty Town, even someone who hadn't been given the brain surge might well have wound up bubbleheaded, just from all the champagne.

Perhaps new-pretty culture is best summed up by the language they spoke (see "Glossary"). In particular, new pretties reduced the huge number of words meaning "good" and "bad" to only two: "bubbly" and "bogus." They could have whole conversations using hardly any other words, which shows how empty-headed the operation had made them. (Oddly, however, since the mind-rain, more people of all ages have started to use pretty-talk. What is it about acting like a bubblehead that's so much fun?)

NOTE: *In many cities, new pretties lived in mansions named after natural pretties of history. (Rusty film stars like Greta Garbo and Rudy Valentino, and pre-Rusty beauties like Claudia Pulchra of ancient Rome and Ono no Komachi of ancient Japan.)*

MIDDLE PRETTIES

After several years the initial effects of the brain surge would fade, and most people would become bored with New Pretty Town's distractions. They would then take a series of exams and upper-level courses to determine what jobs they would hold as an adult.

People who had been tricky as uglies and who had resisted the brain surge as new pretties—in other words, those who had caused the most trouble—were marked for special jobs requiring fast reactions, aggression, and independent thinking. They were given an operation that reversed some or all of the bubblehead effect, then were trained as wardens, firefighters, Rangers, and emergency-room surgeons.

In cities like Diego, the pretties with the greatest resistance to social programming and brain surge often became teachers and librarians. It is believed that this tradition of putting independent thinkers in charge of education led to that city's adoption of the first New System. But in other places, troublemakers were streamed into secret government agencies (see "Special Circumstances"). In Tally Youngblood's city, over time this led to a more and more repressive government.

Once they were assigned jobs, middle pretties moved from New Pretty Town into the suburbs outside the inner-city areas. They were allowed to marry and have children, and lived in single-family houses rather than dorms. As they aged they would have minor operations to change their appearance, replacing beauty and youth with markers of wisdom and authority.

LATE PRETTIES

At age eighty or so, most people retired and moved to Crumblyville. This circle of assisted-living estates lay at the outer reaches of the city, past the factory belt at the border of the wild. Because life-extension surge kept late pretties alive into their middle-hundreds, this ring of estates was growing even before the current Expansion.

—◆—

NOTE: *The term "crumblies" was used to mean late pretties but could also mean anyone older than the speaker. For example, uglies often referred to their parents as "my crumblies," even if technically they were middle pretties.*

CLIQUES

Theoretically, all pretties get along with one another. But in any large group of human beings, there are different types of people who want to spend their time in different ways. So it didn't take long for cliques to form in Tally's city, organized around all the typical new-pretty activities: ballooning, partying, and other kinds of socializing.

Also, it made sense to me that pretties would form cliques. That's the sort of thing that the pretties I knew in high school liked to do.

So here are mini histories of all the cliques mentioned in the Uglies series. (At least, I hope I got them all.)

TALLY'S CITY

Crims

Being crim can change the world.

—MIKI

The Crims are one of the few cliques that started in Uglyville, about a year before Shay and Tally met. That group ran away to the Smoke, except for Zane and Shay, who chickened out. Zane restarted the clique in New Pretty Town, where Tally later joined. As Tally and Zane become famous for their bubbly exploits, the Crims expanded to become one of the largest cliques in New Pretty Town. Many of these new members wound up as Cutters under Shay's guidance (see "Cutters").

The Crims are most famous for their mass balloon escape from New Pretty Town, and although Zane was soon recaptured, he returned to find the Crims still thriving. Tricks and other forms of rebellion had at last become a part of pretty culture. The Crims became a vital conduit between Tally's city and the New Smoke, distributing the cure to tens of thousands of new and middle pretties. Once Dr. Cable was finally ousted from power, many Crims became, ironically, part of the new political leadership of Tally's city.

But by that time, Zane, the Crims' founder, was dead, a tragic victim of the Diego War.

Cutters

The Cutters were my pride and joy, my special *Specials.*

—DR. CABLE

The Cutters were originally a pretty clique started by Shay. When she saw how Tally and Zane were becoming less pretty-minded, Shay tried to create a cure for herself. But the only thing that reduced her bubblehead haze was the extreme pain of cutting. She spread the practice to a few other Crims, including Ho and Tachs, and to many other pretties who had not been voted into the Crims. Together they became the Cutters.

After the Crims' mass escape, the Cutters were recruited by Dr. Cable to become a new division of Special Circumstances. After undergoing her brainwashing, they were dedicated to hunting down the New Smoke. They lived in the wild, even hunting animals for food. In a way, the Cutters lived a twisted version of the Smokey life that Shay had been torn away from (thanks to Tally). Many of the Crims recaptured after the mass escape, including Tally, were given the surgical procedure that turned them into Cutters.

Just before the Diego War, the Cutters were

infiltrated by Fausto—a former member who had been captured and cured by the Smokies—and he cured all of them. In their new form, they became the heroes of the Diego War and have since helped the New Special Circumstances in many missions against cities that expand too far. They no longer cut, but the name remains.

Hot-Airs

If Shay hadn't introduced her to the Crims, Tally figured she would have been a Hot-air. They were always drifting off into the night and landing at random places, calling a hovercar to pick them up from some distant suburb or even past the city limits.

Hot-airs are obsessed with ballooning and all forms of flight. They hate to be on the ground, and even when they aren't in balloons, they prefer to be on balconies or rooftops, and they always live on high floors. They call everyone who isn't a Hot-air a "groundling." As the cure spread through Tally's city, a few Hot-airs took up hoverboarding, a pastime previously unheard of in pretty culture. After the mind-rain, many Hot-airs joined the Extras' space colonization project. Some still prefer the traditional hot-air balloon, and vast fleets can be seen taking off from the cities, filling the night sky with wild colors and tiny spigots of flame.

The Swarm

Of course the Swarm was everywhere, all jabbering to one another on their interface rings.

The Swarm is a tight-knit clique that uses skintenna surge to create social bonds. Their skintennas are all on one shared channel, so that anything one Swarmer says is heard by all the others. They go places only in huge groups and generally don't talk to anyone outside the Swarm. Because of the lack of privacy, the Swarm has lots of infighting, and several groups have broken off from the main clique. To make things confusing, they *all* call themselves the Swarm. All claim to be the original group, and nobody knows which one really is. Since the mind-rain, the Swarm has started to experiment with group-think software, hoping one day to hear one another's *thoughts*. It is unclear how the clique will evolve if they ever get that to work.

Bashers

A mostly naked clique of Bashers were pretending to be pre-Rusties, building bonfires and drumming, establishing their own little satellite party, which was what Bashers always did.

Bashers are an all-male clique who like to drum and who often camp in pleasure gardens rather than living in mansions. Since the mind-rain, many Bashers have joined the pre-Rusty societies kept in reservations by the scientists of Tally's city, trying to recapture their true primitive maleness.

Twisters

. . . Twisters as sick puppies wearing big cone-shaped plastic collars.

Twisters are the most perverse clique in New Pretty Town, doing outrageous things like making themselves look ugly for parties. They throw impromptu drum-machine bashes where people wear horrible masks: devils, scary clowns, monsters, and aliens. (We first meet them in the opening chapter of *Uglies*.) Since the mind-rain, most Twisters have become major surge-monkeys.

Naturals

Tally stumbled into a clique of Naturals plastered with brittle leaves, walking last days of autumn who shed yellows and reds as she shoved through them.

Naturals are pretties who are into gardening and camping. Not as adventurous as Rangers, certainly, but more likely to go into the wild than a normal pretty—though they always bring along lots of champagne.

ASIAN CLIQUES

Of course, cliques are different in every city and region. To completely understand the world of *Extras*, you should probably know a little about the social forces in that part of the world. So here are a few of the cliques that appeared in Asia after the mind-rain.

Youngblood Cults

Great, another cult of me. Just what the world needs.

—TALLY

The importance of fame in Aya's city, combined with the fact that Tally is the most famous person in the world, has led to the rise of the so-called Youngblood Cults. Some of these cliques are simply historical clubs, trying to learn what they can about Tally as a revolutionary and as a person. Other cults, however, are more focused on surging to look like Tally did when she was an ugly, a pretty, or a Special. They seem to have forgotten that Tally's true message is one of self-determination, not hero-worship and imitation.

Sly Girls

You Sly Girls don't cry when you watch the big-face parties on the feeds, just because you weren't invited. You don't stay friends with people you hate, just to bump your face rank. And even though nobody knows what you're doing out here, you don't feel invisible at all.

—AYA

The Sly Girls are an all-female secret clique dedicated to doing tricks *without* becoming famous. The clique was started by Ai (last name unknown), but the Sly Girls' official leader is whoever has the lowest face rank at any given moment. Although the Girls are personally anonymous, their tricks, like bridge jumping and mag-lev surfing, made them famous as a group, and their name became synonymous with mysterious forces at work in the world—like gremlins or faeries.

After Aya Fuse's story that featured them kicked, the Sly Girls became annoyingly famous and had to relocate to another city for a while. But they were soon recognized (for their tricks, not their Plain Jane faces) and became famous there as well. Now they are reconciled to their fame, though they disappear from the public view for long periods of time. And they are rumored to be working on a *really* big trick.

Manga-Heads

Maybe Frizz's intense gaze made everyone feel this way. His eyes were so huge, *just like the old Rusty drawings that manga-heads based themselves on.*

Manga was one of the great popular art forms of the Rusty era, so it isn't surprising that after the mind-rain, many people wanted to look like manga characters. Small noses, big smiles, and huge eyes are the main characteristics of manga-heads, and some sport gravity-challenging hairstyles as well. (Note: Manga-heads are split into many subcliques, depending on the style of the source material.)

Radical Honesty

So let me get this straight, Aya-chan. You want me, a person who can't lie, to lie about the fact that I can't lie?

—FRIZZ

To solve his own problem with truth-slanting, a manga-head named Frizz Mizuno requested that city surgeons perform a new type of brain surge on him, one that eliminated his capacity to lie. A side effect of the operation was that he had to share everything about his life on his feed, which made him a very popular kicker, and this in turn spread the popularity of his surgery. Frizz ultimately reversed the surge, preferring to rely on his own willpower to tell the truth, but his clique, Radical Honesty, is still growing in popularity. Offshoot cliques include Radical Hilarity, Radical Loyalty, and Radical Niceness.

Extras

Every change we've made adapts us better to our future home. We're the first extraterrestrial people.

—UDZIR

The Extraterrestrials (generally known as Extras) originated in Southeast Asia. Founded by an environmentalist named Udzir, they have been planning for space colonization since the beginning of the Expansion, slowly altering themselves to live in a zero-g environment. They also are dedicated to moving much of the metal in the Rusty Ruins into space, both to use as building materials and to slow down the Expansion of the cities. Their major surgical alterations include: replacing their legs with an extra set of arms, moving their eyes for wider peripheral vision, and removing the pigment from their skin for improved vitamin D production with minimal sunlight. Their headquarters is in the ruin of the ancient Rusty city of Singapore, but most Extras now live in space in a group of orbital habitats that they call the New Expansion.

Randoms

Randoms reject all forms of surgery and gene therapy no matter how old and broken-down they get. They believe that life-extension treatments are leading to overpopulation and that no one should live for more than a hundred years. But a surprising number of them change their minds in later life. . . .

Tech-Heads

As the mind-rain unleashes creativity, more people are becoming interested in innovative technologies.

The clique system is the best way to share resources and new ideas. The tech-heads are actually a loose confederation of cliques, including Inventors, Physics Otaku, NeoFoodies, and Mag-Lev Spotters. Recently, many tech-heads have joined the Extras in space.

Reputation Bombers

The Reputation Bombers are a tech-head clique devoted to figuring out how the city's fame algorithms work. They experiment every night by bombing— chanting a different member's name in hope of boosting his or her face rank. Most of their members fade back into oblivion after being bombed, but a few have become permanently famous, because they turned out to be really interesting people once everyone got to know them. The city council has set up a permanent committee, the Fame Spam Board, to fight this and other abuses of the face-rank algorithms. Spin-off groups include Slam Bombers and Hovercam Bombers.

Immortals

A new cult first made famous by Aya Fuse's brother, Hiro, Immortals believe that the technology exists to enable human beings to live forever. Their lawsuit against the global government has in fact turned up evidence that many untried life-extension treatments exist, and that people can live into their mid–two hundreds. Where we're going to put everyone is less clear.

Plain Janes

The Plain Janes are an all-female group who reject all cosmetic surgery, makeup, and hairstyling. Unlike Randoms, they're okay with eyescreens and health modifications, just not with things that would make them pretty. (I stole the name from Cecil Castellucci's excellent graphic novel of that title.)

NeoFoodies

NeoFoodies are tech-heads who experiment with food, separating flavors from structure and using unexpected processes. (And they're real! See "Miscellany.")

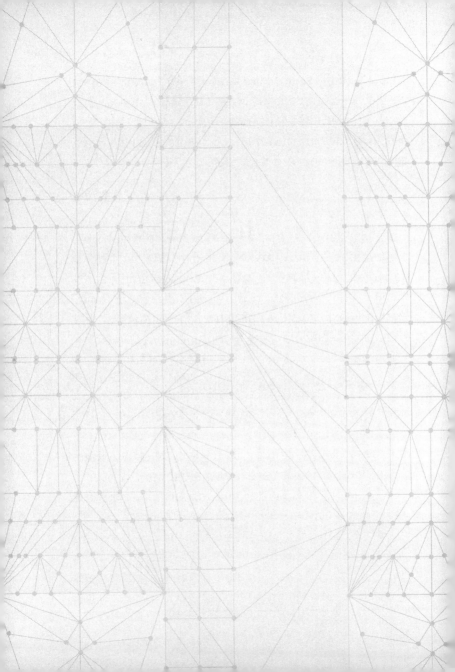

SCIENCE #1:
THE SCIENCE OF BEAUTY

The big eyes and lips said: I'm young and vulnerable, I can't hurt you, and you want to protect me. And the rest said: I'm healthy, I won't make you sick. And no matter how you felt about a pretty, there was a part of you that thought: If we had kids, they'd be healthy too. I want this pretty person. . . .

In ancient Greece it was all about the math.

They believed that beauty had a ratio: roughly 1.618 to 1. The Greeks called this ratio *phi* and used it obsessively in their architecture and art. Temples like the Parthenon and the Acropolis have *phi* all over them. And so does George Clooney's face.

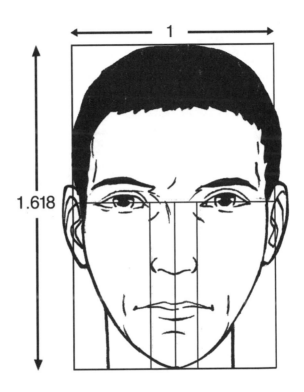

That's right. In many beautiful people, *phi* can be found in the ratio between the width and the height of the head.

Actually, *phi* appears in lots of places on the human body. Another example was made famous by Leonardo da Vinci—the ratio between the distance from the bottom of the feet to the belly button and the distance from the belly button to the top of the head.

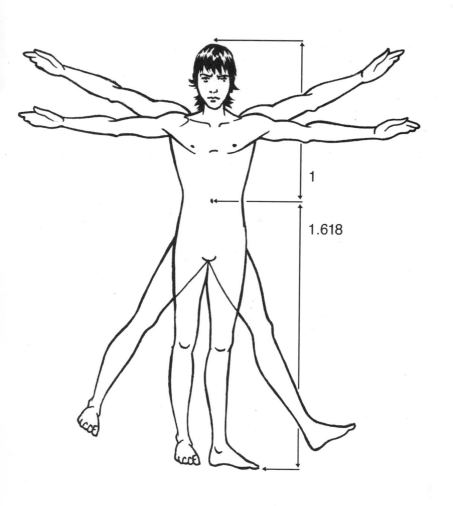

And it's not just people; the rest of nature loves *phi* too. The spirals in seashells, the markings on butterfly wings, and even the needles of pine trees all gravitate toward *phi*. Math geeks have been looking for examples of this ratio for the last few thousand years, claiming to find it in everything from the Great Pyramid to the Mona Lisa.

But don't go measuring the height of your belly button just yet. Modern science doesn't really support *phi* as the magic source of human beauty. Our brains are much more complicated than that. The way we see beauty has more to do with messy stuff like social history and evolution.

But the Greeks' ideas weren't totally bogus. They were right on one important point: You can do math about beauty. Or to put it another way, there are mathematical similarities among the faces that most of us like. None of these findings are strong enough to be called a theory (which is the gold standard in science), but there are many solid hypotheses.

Here are the ones I used when writing *Uglies*.

THE SYMMETRY HYPOTHESIS

Yeah, well, I happen to like my right side. Looks tougher.

—SHAY

In *Uglies*, when Shay and Tally are making morphos of themselves, they start by picking one side of their face, then folding it over. This is called "bilateral symmetry," an exact match between the left and right sides of the face.

The symmetry hypothesis is the strongest mathematical measure of beauty discovered so far. People from dozens of countries have been quizzed about computer-generated photos, and majorities everywhere prefer symmetry. Even babies stare longer at symmetrical faces than uneven ones, and this tendency seems to go beyond just us humans. Female zebra finches and swallows tend to choose males with symmetrical markings over those without. (And note that birds aren't influenced by fashion magazines—they have *no idea* they're supposed to be hot for symmetry.)

So why is symmetry so popular? The answer is simple: It indicates a strong immune system. Being sick when you're a littlie knocks the growing process out of whack, and your features wind up slightly uneven. And evolution wants us to find mates who've been healthy their whole lives. We also don't want to hang out with people who might sneeze and make *us* sick.

Of course, illness happens to all of us; no one in human history ever grew up completely perfect and symmetrical. But somewhere deep in our brains, a lot of us are looking for that morpho that Tally and Shay made—a perfect balance of left and right.

THE AVERAGING HYPOTHESIS

When we say someone has "average looks," that's usually not a good thing. But the math says otherwise.

In 1994, researchers in Scotland used software to "average" dozens of female faces. The computers blended real faces together, creating mathematical composites of their features. When they tested the results, most people found the averaged faces prettier than the originals.

Since then, studies in several countries have backed up the averaging hypothesis. And the more faces that are added to the mix, the prettier the averaged faces become. But why would *averageness* be desirable?

One explanation is that we're all looking for a mix of features in our mates. That is, we want someone who has genes from all parts of the gene pool. Such people would presumably have a wider collection of inherited traits—in other words, useful stuff that we want our own children to have.

An intriguing part of this research is that when people look for beauty, they seem to average their entire community. *All* the faces they see go into the mix. Back when humans lived in tiny villages, that meant only a few hundred people. But these days, we see images of faces from all over the world.

FAQ 1: *Does everyone look the same in Tally's city?*

Answer: *No. There are parameters to keep everyone within certain limits, but you can still tell people apart.*

FAQ 2: *Is there racial variation in Tally's world?*

Answer: *Yes. Each city has its own averaging group, so a city in Asia, like Aya's, would have predominantly Asian features in the mix. Tally's city is on the Pacific coast of North America, so the mix would include Hispanic, African, Asian, and Anglo groups.*

THE NEOTENY HYPOTHESIS

Throughout most of history, people didn't live very long.

Our Neanderthal ancestors only lived to be about twenty. A thousand years ago, the average person made it to thirty. And even a century ago, life expectancy wasn't much more than forty, just over half of what it is now.

This leads to a disturbing fact: For the majority of our evolutionary history, it has been a *really stupid idea* to start a family with someone who was over the age of twenty. Because, not too long ago, that was really old, so your mate wouldn't be around long enough to help you raise your kids. Bad move.

But thanks to social and technological changes,

these days it's the other way around—it's a crazy idea to start a family with anyone *under* twenty. Young people rarely have the resources, education, or experience needed to raise kids. This conflict between evolutionary programming and social reality causes many of the conflicts of being a modern-day teenager. (But that's another book. Um, make that *ten* books.)

This mixed-up situation also leads to the neoteny hypothesis: After age twenty or so, looking younger makes you more attractive.

To reiterate: Our mental wiring hasn't caught up with present-day reality. We *think* that everyone should look twenty, because for eons *that was middle age*.

So what does "young" look like? Well, that's easy to figure out from the tricks we use to make ourselves beautiful. Most of them are related to neoteny.

Full Lips

From age twenty-five or so, the body loses collagen, which is the stuff that makes your lips plump. Lipstick and lip gloss make the lips look bigger. And cosmetic surgeons, of course, will inject collagen into your lips, making them genuinely bigger (and kind of weird-looking, if you ask me).

Full and Lustrous Hair

As you get older, your hair gets thinner (mine does, anyway) and less shiny. Hair extensions, hair growth stimulants and procedures, as well as endless hair products are all used to manipulate your hair back to its youthful fullness and luster.

Big Eyes

Our eyeballs grow faster than the rest of us, so young people's eyes are big in comparison to the rest of their bodies. That's why eyeliner and false eyelashes make us look younger. No one's figured out yet how to make eyes *actually* bigger, but the surgery in Tally's world does exactly that. (Especially for manga-heads!)

Clear and Smooth Skin

Obviously, being a teenager is no picnic when it comes to your skin. But by age twenty, most people have clear, unwrinkled skin. Tricks like concealer, chemical peels, and face-lifts all help to keep it looking that way.

In Tally's world, these markers of youth are present in every new pretty. The operation makes them into exaggerated-looking twenty-year-olds, and keeps them that way for as long as possible. It's not until they start having kids (at about age fifty in Tally's city) that the middle-pretty operation gives them gray hair and a few wrinkles to make them look wise.

FAQ: *Why aren't littlies ugly?*

Answer: *Another feature of neoteny is that we're programmed to protect little kids. So littlies aren't considered ugly in Tally's world—they're too cute and innocent and small. Like penguins.*

THE EXPOSURE EFFECT

Way back in 1968, a social scientist named Robert Zajonc discovered the "exposure effect." Basically, we're all attracted to things that we recognize: a comfortable old T-shirt, a familiar brand of toothpaste, an actor we've seen in a dozen movies. We like what we already know.

This effect also extends to human desire. If someone looks like an old friend of ours, we're more likely to find him or her attractive. And if a person resembles the classic beauties of our culture, we're preprogrammed to believe that they too must be beautiful. In this way, beauty is cultural. That is, people who are considered beautiful in one country may not be considered so in another.

Of course, in Tally's world *everyone* is familiar. The Pretty Committee sets a very narrow range for the operation, so no one looks strange or disturbing. That's one of the reasons why pretties like and trust one another: Nobody seems like an outsider (except, of course, those annoying little uglies).

In Aya's city the exposure effect is even more important. The "big faces" are the people who are the most familiar, because they're on the feeds all the time. As Aya thinks one morning:

> *People's faces were so different since the mind-rain, the new fads and cliques and inventions so unpredictable. It made the city sense-missing sometimes. Famous people were the cure for that randomness, like pre-Rusties gathering around their campfires every night, listening to the elders. Humans needed big faces around for comfort and familiarity, even an ego-kicker like Nana Love just talking about what she'd had for breakfast.*

The exposure effect is also good news for those of us who weren't born gorgeous. It means that the people who know us best—our parents and children, our best friends and true loves—ultimately "forget" what we look like. How symmetrical or clear-skinned we are disappears into the experiences we've shared with someone. After a certain point, it's just like David said to Tally: "What you do, the way you think, makes you beautiful."

THE HALO EFFECT

One of the worst things about focusing on looks is the "halo effect," the tendency to think that pretty people are better than the rest of us. Studies show that attractive people have more friends, get better grades, and make more money. A recent study even suggested that kids who are prettier at age fifteen are less likely to get in serious trouble by the time they're eighteen.

The halo effect invokes a lot of tricky questions: Are people successful because they're pretty? Or do they become pretty because they're successful? Did those pretty kids act up and get away with stuff because of their looks? Or do people who aren't pretty get treated badly, and strike back in ways that get them into trouble?

These are all tough questions. You can almost see why a society like Tally's would finally throw up their hands and say, "Forget it! Let's just make everyone pretty!" They extended the halo effect to everyone, in hopes of a better world.

Clearly they were wrong to make everyone bubbleheaded, but you have to admit that Tally's culture understood one thing: A world in which people treat one another with attention and respect is one with more success, less crime, and more happiness.

THE GOOD NEWS

We're not freaks, Tally. We're normal. We may not be gorgeous, but at least we're not hyped-up Barbie dolls.

—SHAY

One thing you should remember about all this stuff: These hypotheses are about what *most* people are attracted to. There is no "ideal beauty," no single look that everyone in the world loves.

Actually, the thing that Americans obsess about the most—weight—varies widely as a beauty marker. Different cultures find people of different sizes sexy. Even U.S. culture had very different standards of skinniness just a few decades ago. My guess is that the people in Tally's era would find a lot of our current-day movie stars freakishly thin and unhealthy-looking.

And here's another cool discovery: Scientists have found that humans vary as "seers" of beauty. Some people hardly react at all when they see a beautiful face. Like David, they're focused on other things besides looks. (There's actually some evidence that men with high testosterone levels are the biggest suckers for a pretty face, but that seems just *too obvious* to be true.)

Another important point is that almost all beauty studies use photographs. In other words, these "beauties" weren't talking or even moving. I don't know about you, but I'm usually talking or moving when I get to know someone. And yet we have very little scientific data about how personality compares to beauty when it comes to attraction. My guess is that for anyone really worth knowing, what you look like comes in a distant second to a good sense of humor.

And here's one last piece of good news I discovered when researching the averaging hypothesis: There's a difference between pretty and gorgeous. People may find averaged faces attractive as a whole, but the *most* beautiful faces tend to be non-average in some way. So looking weird can be a whole other kind of attractive that's hard to pin down with statistics.

That's why I quoted Francis Bacon in Part II of *Uglies*: "There is no excellent beauty that hath not some strangeness in the proportion."

And that also brings me to a secret never revealed in the books: Another reason for the operation was to get rid of the *truly* beautiful people by burying them in a sea of pretty sameness.

GADGETS AND INVENTIONS

I get asked a lot where the futuristic inventions in *Uglies* come from. How did I get all these crazy ideas? Well, I mostly didn't. Only a few of Tally's gadgets are original to me. Most have a long history in science fiction, and a couple already exist in the here and now. Just so you know which is which, here are a few notes explaining where these gadgets come from and, more important, how likely they are to be a part of *your* future.

COMMUNICATIONS

Hi, ping-la!

—TALLY

The City Interface

The city interface is more or less what we call the Internet—a repository of information available to anyone at any time, and a communication hub for people throughout the world. The main difference is that in Tally's world, the city authorities use the interface to closely watch their citizens. Especially those who are trying to change the system. Actually, this part of Tally's world is slowly coming true in our own world, though the issues of privacy are still being hashed out in the courts. Probably, your generation will be the one to decide whether the "security" of having a government that knows everything about everyone is worth having no privacy.

Interface Ring

Having an interface device is so important in Tally's world, I figured that a ring would make the most sense. It's the easiest accessory to wear and the hardest to lose. Also, a lot of the things the city interface does for Tally—bringing food, opening doors—seem like magic to us. Since rings are associated with magic, I figured that an interface ring would feel right to a present-day reader. Ring-size cell phones are probably not too far away in our world.

Interface Bracelet

Of course, escaping the city interface is fairly easy for most people in Tally's city: You just take off your ring. This was fine for most pretties, who wouldn't think of being miscreants. But when Zane and Tally started causing trouble, I figured the city would have to have a way to keep track of them permanently. I decided on an interface bracelet that could not be removed. One main reason: "Bracelets" is slang for handcuffs.

Skintenna

I partly invented skintennas because it's fun to say "skintenna." I also liked the idea that the Specials were a tight-knit tribe who could hear one another's breathing and were all listening to the same music all the time. The music idea came from reading about a nightclub in London where everyone wears radio headphones. All the headphones play the same music, so it seems like a normal nightclub until you take off your headphones, and see everyone dancing to . . . silence. That struck me as kind of futuristic and a bit uncanny, which is how I wanted the Specials to seem.

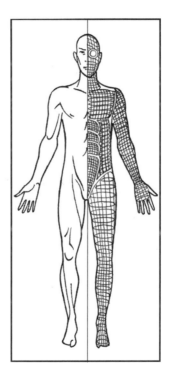

Eyescreen

My dentist gives me these eyeglasses that have little screens in them, so I can watch a movie while he works on me. It's very weird, like the movie is hovering right in front of me. I figured the media-obsessed people of Aya's city wouldn't want to ever stop watching the feeds, so eyescreens would be totally necessary. Researchers at the University of Washington have already made an eyescreen prototype, but it doesn't show video yet, just simple information on an LED screen. Aya's eyescreen doesn't use glasses or contact lenses—the device is placed inside her eyeballs with surgery. It feeds data from the city interface directly into her optic nerve and coordinates with other devices in her ears (to add audio data), jaw (for voice commands and speech communication), and fingers (for gestural control).

Tracker Locket

The tracker that Tally takes to the Smoke could have looked like anything, but a locket seemed the most dramatic to me. Usually lockets carry pictures of loved ones, so Tally's makes everyone assume that she has a boyfriend back in the city. But in fact the locket symbolizes someone she hates—Dr. Cable—and she winds up hurting David with it. Ah, delicious irony.

HOVERING STUFF

All that glitters is not hovery.

—SHAY

> **Note:** *For the science of hovering and mag-lev trains, see "Magnetic Levitation." For hoverboards, see "Hover-board Manual."*

Hovercar

The hovercar concept is an old one in science fiction. (The *Oxford English Dictionary* traces the word back to 1960.) I figured Tally's world needed hovercars, because middle pretties would never use boards. Cars are much easier to fly, they keep you out of the weather, and there's room for your littlies. New pretties would probably use hovercars too, because they're too simple-minded to use hoverboards. But then again, they never leave New Pretty Town!

Hovercars have actually existed in our world for decades now, but they use lifting rotors instead of magnetic levitation. (See "Science #2: Magnetic Levitation" to learn why.)

Bungee Jacket

Pretties are always doing stupid things, but Tally's society is obsessed with safety, so I figured that they'd need a lot of bungee jackets around to keep pretties from getting hurt. More important, bungee jackets allow my heroes to jump off tall things and not die, which is very useful for an author.

Bungee jackets would probably be very hard to create with present-day technology. A magnet strong enough to catch a falling person would be too heavy to wear. And, of course, you'd have to build a grid everywhere to use them. But there's always regular bungee jumping!

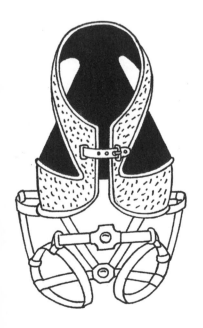
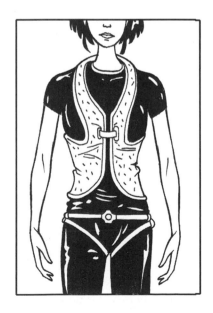

Floating Ice Rink

I have no idea where this idea came from, except that it allowed me to write a scene that put together my three favorite things: fireworks, falling, and miscreant behavior. Could anyone build a floating ice rink? Perhaps the real question is *why* would they? Still, it's exactly the sort of pretty, useless thing that Tally's culture loves.

Special Hoverboard

I liked that the escaped uglies had to follow rivers to travel by hoverboard, but I figured Specials would get bored of that. So I decided to come up with a hoverboard with lifting fans for off-grid use. Basically, it's like standing on a miniature double-rotor helicopter. In our world, it's likely that a Special-style hoverboard will be created before the magnetic kind. It'll be very loud, though, and probably dangerous.

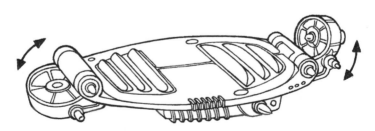

Hoverball Rig

After the mind-rain made everyone clever, I figured that more people would start inventing stuff. So somebody *had* to create a way to fly without a board, and then a sport to go with it! The hoverball rig started as just background for Hiro's character, but I gradually realized that the Extras would use them to simulate zero-g. It's cool how inventions that start out just for fun often wind up as part of the plot.

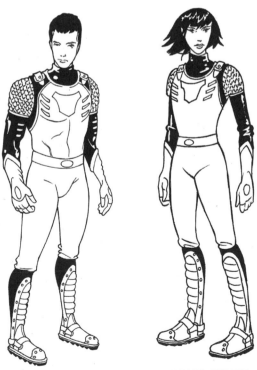

Hovercam

Here's why I created Moggle, Aya's hovercam: Aya spends a lot of time on her own, a scenario that tends to bog down a story. Two characters can talk and argue about what's going on, but one lone character can only argue with herself, which gets silly after a while. So I decided that a sidekick would help Aya's solo scenes. Even though Moggle doesn't say anything, the hovercam gives Aya someone to talk to and worry about. In a way, Moggle also shows how lonely Aya is, because Aya cares more about fame than friends.

> *Note: Hovercams first appear in* Pretties. *But it didn't occur to me that a hovercam could be a character until I created the media-obsessed world of* Extras.

SURVIVAL EQUIPMENT

"I thought that food of the gods would be . . . better, somehow."

"Hey, this is dehydrated *food of the gods, okay?"*

—ANDREW AND TALLY

Whenever I go into a camping store, I marvel at all the cool stuff: GPS devices, Mylar blankets, and clothing made from futuristic materials. It's funny that some of the most advanced technology we use is for . . . getting back to nature. I wanted the Smokies to have some of that contradiction in their society. They're products of an advanced civilization, even if they do live in the wild, so I gave them lots of cool toys. But because camping technology is so advanced, most of the stuff they use is available today!

Self-Heating Food

The U.S. military has been eating MREs (Meals Ready to Eat) for decades. A reporter friend of mine brought one back from Iraq, and it was really weird. When she set it off, it hissed and sputtered and steamed, cooking the food inside with a chemical reaction (like a really powerful glow stick). I created a quieter, more sophisticated version for Tally to eat in the wild, but it's basically the same trick.

Water Purifier

People can go without food for a long time, but not without water. A water purifier would be the one device that would make long-term camping much simpler. It looks like a normal water cup but has electronics inside that separate impurities from the water. These impurities wind up in a "muck-trap" in the bottom. We don't have any technology like this now, but there are pills you can drop into water to purify it. (And, hey, boiling works too.)

Position-Finder

This is basically just a GPS device. So common, your phone may have one.

SURGERY

Sometimes I think I'm nothing but what other people have done to me—a big collection of brainwashing, surgeries, and cures.

—TALLY

Surge Tank

It took me until the end of writing *Specials* to realize that Tally *had* to wake up in a surge tank at least once. Her character is changed so many times by operations, I needed to show the physical reality and horror of the actual process. Plus, it was dramatic to have Tally *literally* break out of the cycle of surgery that she was trapped in.

Surge tanks are very common in science fiction movies, of course. There's something about floating in water that's like going back to the womb, making regeneration seem almost like a rebirth. Maybe that's where I got the notion that all my characters are "reborn" after surgery.

In the present day, doctors use "physiologic saline tanks" to preserve tissues while they're waiting to transplant them. A future surge tank would probably be based on these.

Flash Tattoos

The tattoos on the cover of *Specials* were inspired by those worn by Maori tribesmen. (The Maori are the people who got to New Zealand about six hundred years before the Europeans did.) But moving tattoos are much more recent. The first "subcutaneous display" (an electronic flash tattoo in our world) was part of a cell phone system designed by John Mielke in 2008. The weird thing is, it's powered by blood sugar.

> **Note:** *For more than a century, the word "flash" has meant a badge sewn onto a uniform, and flash tattoos were sort of a uniform for the Crims. Also, the term "flash tattoo" goes back to at least 1977, when it referred to mass-produced tattoo templates, like the classic heart and snake designs. I like it when my slang terms have historical bases like these do.*

Eye Surge

So wait. You have jewels in your eyes? And they tell time? And they go backward? *Isn't that maybe* one *thing too many, Shay?*

—TALLY

If you want eye surge like Shay's, just head over to Holland. There, the Netherlands Institute for Innovative Ocular Surgery will happily implant jewelry in the whites of your eyes. These little silver shapes—hearts, clovers—won't tell time, but they will freak out your friends and family.

Note: *Most eye doctors are against this procedure. And, for the record, so am I.*

WEAPONS

They're just lucky we didn't use nanos.

—SHAY

Needle Ring

Poison rings are really old—the Medici family used them to kill their political opponents in Florence five hundred years ago! But the Medicis' rings carried poison in hidden compartments, to dump into someone's food or drink. So far I can't find any examples in history of rings with tiny needles. But they would probably look like the illustration below:

Little Men

I think these little guys were the result of watching *The Blair Witch Project*. Crude little man-shapes made from straw or sticks are always totally scary to me. And I thought that their evil magic actually being high-tech neural jammers would be cool.

Sneak Suit

The Specials' sneak suits use "active camouflage," which means they change like a chameleon to match their background. This technology is screaming along these days, so quickly that sneak suits may exist in the near future. Scientists are already working on an "invisibility cloak" that takes the light hitting you from one side and passes it around you to the other side. The problem is, you have to stand completely still for this technology to work. (The Cutters could move and still be invisible.)

Present-day camouflage technology uses "organic light-emitting diodes," borrowing techniques from living cells to change color. That's because octopuses and cuttlefish are way ahead of humans in this game. They can change their entire skin to mimic whatever surface they're hiding against. Cuttlefish can even reproduce checkerboards on their skin. Search YouTube for "octopus camouflage" and you will be totally freaked out. (That person sitting next to you? Secretly an octopus.)

Note: *People who are color-blind are better at seeing through camouflage than the rest of us.*

Glitterbomb

In our world glitterbombs are called "flash grenades," designed for hostage situations and other times when you don't want to kill anyone. When they explode, these grenades make a really loud noise (170 decibels to be exact; jet engines

are only 140) and a really bright light. This is enough to stun you for a few minutes, and more than enough to blind a hovercam.

Note: *To read about Hungry Nanos, see "Science #3: Nanos."*

MISCELLANEOUS

The world needed more fireworks—especially now that there was going to be a shortage of beautiful, useless things.

Safety Fireworks

I'm a big sucker for fireworks, and I thought it would make sense for the pretties to have a safe, cool-burning kind to play with. The image of nightly fireworks over New Pretty Town became symbolic of pretty culture. Like pretties, fireworks are silly and a bit useless, but you can't take your eyes off them.

Note: *In* Specials, *when Tally thinks, "The world needed more fireworks—especially now that there was going to be a shortage of beautiful, useless things," it's a reference to the John Ruskin quote from the very beginning of* Pretties: *"Remember that the most beautiful things in the world are the most useless."*

Morphos

In *Uglies*, Tally and Shay create pretty faces to see what they'll look like after their operations. In the real world, plastic surgeons have software so their patients can do pretty much the same thing. (Of course, in real plastic surgery there are no guarantees you'll wind up looking the way you want!)

My morphos were actually inspired by the faces used in beauty studies, "averaged" human faces created by computers. Turn to "Science #1: The Science of Beauty," or Google "virtual Miss Germany" to see a few examples.

Note: *To read about smart matter and the hole in the wall, see "Science #3: Nanos."*

SCIENCE #2:
MAGNETIC LEVITATION

Of course a hoverboard. What is it about those things and miscreants?

—DR. CABLE

Hold two magnets close to each other and you'll see something funny. Oriented one way, they snap together. But if you turn one of them around, the magnets push each other away. That's because every magnet has two poles (called north and south), and no matter where you are in the universe, magnets follow these two simple laws:

1. Opposite poles attract each other.

2. Poles with the same charge repulse each other.

Since humans first noticed them, magnets have been used in countless devices. Pre-Rusty explorers didn't have location finders (no satellites!) so they relied on compasses to show them which way was north (the poles of our planet are also magnets). We Rusties invented electric motors, which use magnets to turn gears and wheels, and we use tiny magnetic switches to store computer data.

But the coolest trick of magnetic forces is something called "magnetic levitation." With powerful enough magnets, you can push anything you want into the air—even a whole train!

MAG-LEV TRAINS

But surfing's more fun *if you're scared.*

—MIKI

Mag-lev trains are one of the few gadgets in the series that are totally real. In fact, the first patent for a mag-lev train was granted in 1902! But that was a bit optimistic. Nobody got a mag-lev train to levitate until 1979, in Germany. Still, mag-levs are older than most *Uglies* fans. . . .

But here's something to remember: Mag-levs only hover a centimeter or two in the air. So what makes them so awesome? Well, because they aren't actually touching their tracks, they don't create any ground friction as they move. This makes them much, much faster than regular trains and almost silent at low speeds.

> **Note:** *Present-day mag-levs go much faster than the ones in Aya's city—as fast as five hundred kilometers per hour. As no one could possibly stand on top of something going that fast, I gave the Sly Girls a slower cargo train to ride. So, in case it wasn't obvious, don't try this at home!*

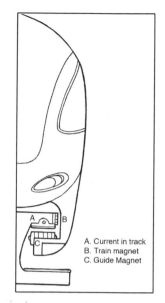

A. Current in track
B. Train magnet
C. Guide Magnet

LEVITATING FROGS

"That's to solve your floating problem."

"I have a floating problem?"

—REN AND AYA

There's one cool kind of technology that I didn't use in *Uglies*. It's called "diamagnetic levitation," and it uses the magnetic properties of the water in your body to push you up. It's like hoverboarding without a board!

Researchers have actually made this work, lifting a frog into the air with no visible means of support. The problem is, floating a frog used sixteen teslas of magnetic force. Um, *teslas*? Well, to give you an idea how much that is, the largest stable magnetic field *ever* produced was about forty-five teslas, barely enough to levitate a cat. And that was in a lab, with a giant generator pumping in the juice.

Making even a few people float using this method would probably eat up all the electricity in a city, so using diamagnetic levitation in *Uglies* would've been pretty bogus. My characters have to stand on (or at least wear) something metal when they fly.

Still, that's one lucky frog.

SUPERCONDUCTORS

Tally laid it flat, stretched out in the sun, where its metallic surface turned jet black as it drank in solar energy. In a few hours it would be charged up and ready to ride again.

The hoverboards that Tally and her friends use are made from superconductors, materials that are near-perfect conductors of electricity. Superconductors also make incredibly strong magnets, and they don't suck power like normal electromagnets.

The fastest experimental mag-lev trains already use superconductors, but there's one problem: Current superconducting materials have to be kept really cold—like, a hundred degrees below zero. That's tricky enough with a massive train, but if you're designing a person-size hoverboard, it's completely nuts. I mean, your board already has to carry the magnets, the control system, and the rider. You don't want to add the weight of a giant refrigerator as well!

Luckily, by the time Tally is born, someone has invented a room-temperature superconductor, one that works in an everyday climate. That's why they can recharge their boards with a low-energy source like solar power. Actually, this is one *Uglies* invention that may not be far off. And when we finally have room-temperature superconductors, they'll revolutionize (and maybe save) our planet by making energy much cheaper and cleaner.

Note: *There has to be some temperature at which the superconducting materials in Tally's world fail and hoverboards stop working. That would have been a good plot point when Tally and David were crossing the desert, but I didn't think of it until just now. Rats.*

For more about how hoverboards work in Tally's world, turn to the chapter "Hoverboard Manual."

NAMES IN THE PRETTYTIME

NEW PRETTY SUFFIXES

Aya looked into Tally's eyes, trying to read her expression. She was pretty sure that –la was a good title. Tally had called her friend Shay-la at least once.

New pretties use the suffixes "-wa" and "-la" only to address someone they are very familiar with, sort of like *tu* instead of *vous* in French.

New pretty suffixes follow two simple rules:

1. If a name has an "l" in it, add "-wa": Tally-wa, Billy-wa.

2. If a name has no "l," add "–la": Shay-la, Aya-la, Zane-la.

Note: *Peris doesn't use "-la" on Tally when she visits him in New Pretty Town, because she's an ugly. Also, her parents don't use it, because middle pretties never talk that way. Dr. Cable uses it once or twice, but only sarcastically, to make Tally feel like a bubblehead again.*

JAPANESE SUFFIXES

I'm honored to meet you, Tally-sama.

—AYA

Part of what inspired me to use suffixes in *Pretties* was my study of Japanese, which uses a complicated set of "honorifics." These suffixes are added to people's names to show how intimate you are with someone, how respected or famous they are, and so on. It made sense that Aya's status-obsessed culture would still use them.

Japanese honorifics are actually quite complicated (to us outsiders, anyway) so I kept the suffixes to just three: "-sama," "-chan," and "-sensei." Here's how those suffixes work in *Extras,* as opposed to modern-day Japanese:

In Aya's city, "-sensei" is used for any one of the city's top thousand most-famous citizens. In real-world Japanese it's used for respected professionals like teachers, doctors, and lawyers. Famous people like manga artists and novelists are called "sensei" by their fans. If you take any martial arts classes, you probably address your teacher as "sensei."

Aya uses "-sama" for world-famous people, like Tally and Shay, who are in all the history books at school. In real-world Japan, "-sama" is used only for very important people. The empresses and princesses of Japan are called "-sama," and Japanese Christians refer to God as *Kami-sama* and Jesus as *Iesu-sama*. But it's not all about divinity. If you go into a store in Tokyo, you may find yourself being called "-sama," which gives you some idea of how good customer service is in Japan.

Finally, Aya's city uses "-chan" for close friends and siblings (particularly if they're younger) and cute machines like Moggle. This is pretty much the way it's used nowadays, though there are more gender issues in present-day Japan than in Aya's city. You probably wouldn't call your male friends "-chan," and even boys' parents stop after a certain age. However, lots of well-loved celebrities are called "-chan," even if they are men. Arnold Schwarzenegger is Shuwa-chan, which is just too cute for words. That's why I decided that Nana Love would be called *Nana-chan*, even though she's famous enough to be a sensei.

UGLIES CHARACTER NAMES

"David? That's a weird name." It sounded made up, to Tally. She decided again that this was all a joke.

Fans often ask me where characters' names come from. Like most writers, I do think a lot about what to call my characters, but there are no hard-and-fast rules. Some are easy, some take months of tinkering to get right. But here's how the major characters of the series got their names. (Those of you who read my blog (scottwesterfeld.com/blog) may have seen some of this before. Sorry.)

Tally Youngblood

Tally's name was an important one. We're stuck inside Tally's head for 240,000 words! Obviously, her name can't be annoying or unwieldy. My original name for her, "Panzercrappitastica Bonechomper," was dropped for this reason. But I had to keep in mind that *Uglies* takes place three hundred years in the future, and after a huge world-wrecking disaster. Names probably wouldn't be the same as they are now.

So I needed something that's not a current name, but that doesn't make your brain go on the fritz when you read it. So I chose a regular word in English:

"tally," as in "count." As in "Banana Boat Song": "Hey, Mr. Tally Man, tally me bananas."

The cool thing about using a real word is that the little spell-checker in your brain doesn't ping every time your eyes scan across those letters. (And the real-world spell-checker doesn't draw a red squiggly line under it.) "Tally" is capitalized, of course, so you know it's a name, but otherwise it reads like a perfectly normal word.

But "tally" isn't *too* common. When's the last time you actually used it in a sentence, like, "Let me tally those Scrabble scores for you, old chum?" Names that are common words are very bad. I suggest to all you budding writers never to name a main character Said, Her, or The.

Actually, it's Tally's last name that's the most interesting. Youngblood is sort of halfway between "Young Turk" (a political upstart) and "fresh blood" (a newcomer). You can tell from the start that Tally is going to disrupt the system. In fact, her last name might have been a bit *too* obvious, except that last names don't get used very often in that world. Usually it's Dr. Cable or some other authority figure who uses her last name, like when your parents yell, "Get back in this house, Scott David Westerfeld!" (Okay, *your* parents don't yell that, but mine did.)

I knew I'd chosen the right last name for Tally in *Pretties*, when the savages who see her as a renegade god fallen from the sky started calling her "Young Blood." It just *fit*.

Shay

Shay is a real name, but it's not very common. If you check the U.S. Social Security baby name rankings (ssa.gov/OACT/babynames/) you'll find that it hasn't cracked the top thousand in the last ten years. It made 981 back in 1995, but that was as a boy's name. In its place of origin, Ireland, it's a girl's name that means "fairy palace."

I'm not sure where in my brain it came from, but I like that it shares two letters with "Tally," because they're more alike than most readers realize.

David

David has the only "normal" name in *Uglies*, and of course he's from outside the system, so he should stick out. Because he grew up in the wild, David's kind of old-fashioned and out-of-place.

And yes, David is my middle name, and I have a tiny scar across one eyebrow. I actually don't know where David got his scar, but I got mine fencing. (Wear the mask, people! That's what it's for.)

Zane

Zane's name started out as "Asher," after a friend of mine's kid. But ultimately I didn't want any city-dwellers to have such normal names. My wife, Justine, suggested Zane, which has the science-fictional *Z* thing going on, so I liked it. It rhymes with "sane," and in both *Pretties* and *Specials*, Zane is Tally's main link to sanity (or at least to her real self, which may or may not be sane).

A lot of fans have written to ask me if I knew that both "Zane" and "David" mean "beloved," because it just makes so much sense. But I had no idea. I'm just lucky that way.

Az and Maddy

I'm not sure where I got the name for David's father. But *"Az"* is recognizable to the eye: we think of *A* and *Z* as the two ends of the alphabet, and "AZ" is the abbreviation for Arizona. Maddy is a name I've used before, a nickname for the character Madeleine in my Midnighters books. I like that it sounds slightly crazy, and Maddy does go a bit crazy after her husband's death (from Tally's point of view, anyway).

Peris

Peris sounds like, but isn't quite, a real place-name: Paris. Again, it's familiar and yet not quite twentieth century. Also, Paris is a mystical city of lights that people fantasize about going to, sort of like New Pretty Town, where we first meet Peris.

> **Trivia:** *In the original outline for the series, Peris was named Peri, another girl. But their first conversation was easier to write using "he" and "she," so I changed Peris's gender. (How lazy is that?) Also, I liked that Tally had a BFF who was a boy, and that it wasn't about romance.*

> **FAQ:** *Were Peris and Tally ever an item?*
>
> **Answer:** *No! Boys and girls* can *be just friends, you know.*

Dr. Cable

Like Peris and Tally, Dr. Cable has a name that is recognizable as a normal word. But "cable" brings to mind electronics and suspension bridges, so it's much more technological and cold than, say, Peris/Paris. Think steel cables and wiry muscles, or all the wires in Dr. Frankenstein's lab.

Andrew Simpson Smith

Like David, Andrew was raised in the wild, so he has an old-fashioned name. Plus I like it that he's a "Smith" even though his people haven't invented iron yet. (Smiths all got their name from being blacksmiths or silversmiths or whatever.) So his name is sort of out-of-time, just like his village.

Part of me finds it amusing that the barbarian is the only character in the trilogy with a middle name, because triple-barreled names sound posh and non-barbarian to me.

An, Sussy, and Dex

Just to remind you: An, Sussy, and Dex are the trio of characters who write "The Smoke Lives!" to create a distraction in *Uglies*. An is a Chinese name (pronounced "ahn"), Dex is short for Dexter, and Sussy rhymes with "fussy." Since these three appeared together, I wanted their names to be different and balanced: one Asian, one European, one purely futuristic.

EXTRAS CHARACTER NAMES

"My name is Aya Fuse."

"No kidding. Every feed in this city seems to know you. And stop bowing!"

—AYA AND TALLY

Unlike the names in the trilogy, most of the character names in *Extras* weren't made up. This is partly because very few of my readers are Japanese, so regular Japanese names were unfamiliar enough. But those of you who read manga may have run into some of these names before. (Before I go on, let me thank fellow novelist and friend Chris Barzak for his help with getting these names right!)

Aya Fuse

Aya was one of the first Japanese names I ever ran into, because the daughter of a dear friend of mine is named Aya. I've always liked the sound of the name, and it was particularly good for the main character of *Extras*, because it sounds so much like "eye." It was also important to me that "Aya-la" sounded good, because I knew that Tally and her gang were going to show up and call her that.

The last name Fuse is also a real Japanese name. I loved that in English a fuse is something you use to start an explosion, because the story that Aya kicks results in many explosions, including a few literal ones. Just so you know, her name is pronounced "FOO-zeh."

Hiro Fuse

English-speaking novelists find it irresistible that there's a Japanese name that sounds just like "hero." In Neal Stephenson's *Snow Crash*, the main character is actually named Hiro Protagonist, which is probably taking things a bit too far. But I liked it as a name for Aya's older brother, because despite being stuck up and annoying, Hiro really is her hero. She idolizes him, and he's probably the reason she got into kicking.

Also, a big chunk of the first draft of *Extras* was written from Hiro's point of view, so he really was the book's hero for a while. (See "Miscellany" for more on this.)

Frizz Mizuno

Frizz is not a real Japanese name. But I wanted one completely made up name, because it is three hundred years in the future, after all. I'm not sure why "Frizz" popped into my head, except that his Radical Honesty makes him the comic relief in the novel, so I thought his name should be something light and, um, frizzy. His last name is real, though.

Ren Machino

Ren is a name you may recognize from the manga series Shaman King, by Hiroyuki Takei. A guy called Ren also appears in Nana, my favorite series. But originally, Ren's name was Rez, which was completely made up. It sounded too much like Frizz, so I changed it.

Ren's last name is also common in Japan, but I used it for its English-language connotations. Ren is good with machines and inventions, so calling him "Machino" was just too good to pass up.

Ai

Wait . . . there's no character named Ai in *Extras*, is there? Well, Ai is the secret real first name of Jai/Kai/Lai, the name-shifting leader of the Sly Girls. Every time she gets too famous, she just sticks another consonant in front. The name Ai will be familiar to readers of *Princess Ai*, which is written by Courtney Love, who I think would probably hang out with my Ai.

> **Note:** *Jai/Kai/Lai's names change* in alphabetical order, *which makes no sense for someone who doesn't even speak English.*

Nana Love

The manga series Nana, by Ai Yazawa, is about two girls with the same name sharing an apartment in Tokyo. It's my favorite manga, so I had to use "Nana" somewhere. Her last name fits perfectly because everyone in the whole city loves her. Yes, you actually can be *that* obvious as a novelist, and no one ever seems to notice.

SLANGUAGE

I've found that there are only two kinds of slang that are any good: slang that has established itself in the language, and slang that you make up yourself. Anything else is apt to be passé before it gets into print.

—RAYMOND CHANDLER,
RAYMOND CHANDLER SPEAKING

I think Chandler is totally right here— you can't use up-to-the-minute slang in a work of fiction, because books take too long to write and publish. So you have to use the classics or make up stuff. Another way is to steal your slang from a faraway place or time. (As you'll see in the glossary, much of the slang in *Uglies* comes from present-day Australia and from 1920s England.)

But *how* do you make up your own slang?

One concept I try to employ when inventing words is called FUDGE. It was created by Allan Metcalf in his book *Predicting New Words*, and explains why some slang sticks around and some disappears. FUDGE stands for:

Frequency of use
Unobtrusiveness
Diversity of users and situations
Generation of other forms and meanings
Endurance of the concept

Frequency of use is important because to get a word stuck in our heads, we have to say it often. When I introduce a new term, I make sure the characters repeat it over the next few pages, just like new vocabulary in a language textbook. Words that mean basic concepts like "good" and "bad" ("bubbly" and "bogus") are the easiest to introduce, because you get lots of chances to use them.

Unobtrusiveness means that the slang word can't be too distracting, because that will just annoy the reader. For example, I love the word "chillaxing" (from "chilling" and "relaxing") but don't see it being used three hundred years from now. It's just too obvious and silly. Most of the slang terms in the series are just ordinary words used in a new way—"icy," "tricks," "crumbly." They're much less obtrusive than made-up words. My favorite of these is "surge," which is both short for "surgery" and also a normal word on its own. (This also means no little red squiggle under it in my word processor.)

Diversity of users and situations is important for any major slang word—think about all the ways we use "lame" or "cool." I used "bubbly" to mean "happy," "stimulating," "good," and even "champagne." And later when Tally is a Special, "bubbleheaded" means stupid and compliant, which shows how much she's changed—happiness has become a foreign concept to her.

Generation of other forms and meanings is part of the glory of slang. Once we have "hoverboard," we can move on to hovercar, hovercam, hoverbounced, hoverskates, hover-lifters, and hoverstruts. This explosion of forms shows the reader how important that technology is to Tally's culture. It also interconnects the different pieces of her world, which makes it all seem more real.

Endurance of the concept simply means that slang about like, love, and happiness will probably last longer than slang about, say, *High School Musical*. That's kind of obvious, so I like to replace Metcalf's *E* in FUDGE with my own . . . euphony.

Euphony means pretty-sounding-ness, and that's the secret key to slang. If a made-up word isn't fun to say, the characters won't sound believable using it. So as I introduce slang into my books, I practice it myself *out loud and in public*, which tends to confuse strangers (and annoy friends). But if a word isn't good enough to say in front of a perplexed shopkeeper, it probably shouldn't exist.

Another part of euphony is making all the slang for one culture sound similar, in the way that Italian words all sound, um, *Italian*. That's why so much of Tally's slang ends in a *y* sound: crumbly, icy, Rusty, bubbly, ugly, pretty. They all sound like they belong together. And as I said earlier, much of the slang in the series was stolen from Australian, which also has lots of words ending in a *y* sound: "brekkie" (breakfast), "stickies" (sweet wines), and even "Chrissie pressies" (take a guess).

Having put all this work into my slang, it's very happy-making when readers tell me that they use pretty-talk at school. It shows that my slang passes the FUDGE test!

FAQ 1: *If the people in Aya's city aren't bubbleheads, why do they use pretty-talk?*

Answer: *Because it's so much fun. Since the mind-rain, people can talk any way they want, after all. So why not enjoy it?*

FAQ 2: *But wait! In Aya's city they speak Japanese, right? So how can they possibly be using phrases like "happy-making"?*

Answer: *I'm glad I made you up so that you could ask that, FAQtoid. The Japanese are particularly enthusiastic about borrowing words from other languages. (They even have a special alphabet for loan words, just to make sure foreign words aren't confused with real Japanese ones.) After Tally became world famous, lots of people in Aya's city started to use pretty-talk borrowed from Tally's city.*

SCIENCE #3:
NANOS

Shay and I had a bad experience with nanos.

—TALLY

Here's the funny thing about fire: a cheery blaze on a cold night will keep you warm, but one stray spark can devour your whole house. Fire can cook your food, or burn your fingers. It's very useful to have around, as long as it doesn't get out of control.

Nanotechnology is a lot like fire. That's why nanos keep popping up in the Uglies series. They can do lots of amazing stuff: heal your body, make clothes appear from a hole in the wall, even change your brain. But they're pretty much guaranteed to cause plot complications.

So what *are* nanos? Well, they're basically machines—*really* small ones.

HOW SMALL IS A NANO?

The word "nano" means "a billionth," so a nanometer is a billionth of a meter. Nanotech machines are between one and one hundred nanometers across. But how small is that?

Often we compare small things to the width of an average human hair. But that's *100,000* nanometers, way too big. A spec of dust is still about a thousand nanometers across. For a truly nanoscale object, we have to zoom down to a strand of your DNA, which is about two nanometers wide.

Obviously, nanos are way too small to see. But enough of them together can become visible. Here's the head of a pin with a thousand medium-size nanos clustered together:

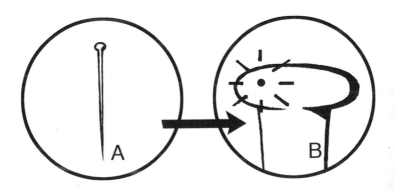

But these things don't exist yet, do they? Isn't this all future stuff? In fact, nanos are pretty old. They go back to the time of moon missions, Pac-Man, and bell bottoms.

ANCIENT NANO HISTORY

The term "nanotechnology" was coined in 1974 by a visionary scientist named Norio Taniguchi. He realized that if individual atoms and molecules could be combined in certain ways, they could work together like the parts of a clock.

But actually, Professor Taniguchi's inspiration came from an even earlier source. Evolution has been using nanos for about 3 billion years. The proteins in your body, like DNA, are basically nanoscale machines. (This close relationship between nanos and life makes some people nervous—but we'll get back to that soon.)

It wasn't until 1985 that anyone actually created a nanoscale object. The first one was called a "fullerine," after an engineer named Buckminster Fuller. Most people just call them "buckyballs," because they look a lot like soccer balls.

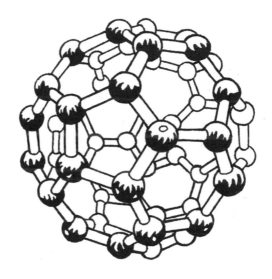

Buckyballs come in all sizes. This one is a single nanometer across and contains sixty carbon atoms. For comparison, your body has about this many carbon atoms in it: 700,000,000,000,000,000,000,000,000.

Scientists are still working out what to *do* with buckyballs. It's sort of like discovering the wheel— to get any use out of it, you still need to invent wheelbarrows, horse carts, and racing cars. But so far buckyballs have shown promise in treating illness, making microscopic batteries, building superhard substances, and conducting electricity. That's a lot of potential for sixty atoms.

SELF-ASSEMBLY AND SELF-REPLICATION

Once humans had built our first buckyballs, something odd happened: We started finding them in nature. They appeared in the soot of trees struck by lightning and in the remains of ancient volcanos. And very "large" buckyballs, up to four hundred carbon atoms, were found wherever meteors hit the earth.

That brings up the coolest thing about nanomachines—the pieces can assemble themselves. Like any chemical process, if you create the right conditions, nanos can happen on their own. Just jolt a pair of carbon rods with electricity, and buckyballs form like magic.

The fact that nanos self-assemble leads to another wonderful, and horrifying, possibility. One day we might be able to create nanos that replicate themselves. Like living cells, nanos could contain the information they need to build a copy of themselves. The advantages would be huge—what if we could invent medicines, clothing, and other useful stuff that would build free copies of themselves?

Everyone wins, right?

Here's the problem: If a nano makes an exact copy of itself, then that copy will *also* make a copy of itself. And that copy will make a copy of *itself* . . .

and so on. If you don't build a limiting factor into your self-replicating nanos, they could wind up devouring the entire world!

This is called the "grey goo" problem, because if the entire planet were turned into copies of a single tiny machine, everything would resemble a featureless goo. Even if the runaway nanos only consumed carbon, that would be enough to kill all carbon-based life forms, which means you, me, and every other living creature in the world.

Most scientists believe that this outcome is unlikely. After all, living creatures have been self-replicating for billions of years, and no bug has yet figured out how to eat the whole planet. But still . . .

NANOS IN TALLY'S WORLD

In Tally's world, nanotechnology is part of everyday life. Because it's so omnipresent, Tally and her friends often don't even notice when they interact with nanos. So here's a full list of all the times nanos pop up:

The Hole in the Wall

Pretties are allowed to have all the cool clothes and toys they could ever want, thanks to the "hole in the wall." When they get tired of anything, they just toss it in the recycler, which breaks it back down to raw material. But where do these clothes come from?

As Hiro explains in *Extras*, the hole in the wall is a self-contained nanotech factory. It turns patterns (called "nano-frames") into physical objects. For example, invisible nanos would weave carbon molecules into threads, which would be programmed to weave themselves together to make clothing.

You can think of the hole in the wall as a kind of three-dimensional printer. These days if you want a photo of a pair of shoes, you can download a photo from the Internet and print it. But in Tally's world you can "print" things in three dimensions, so you can actually print *the shoes themselves*.

FAQ 1: *So why don't uglies have holes in their walls?*

Answer: *To make them even more desperate to have the operation. Clever, huh?*

FAQ 2: *If everyone has a hole, what's the factory belt for?*

Answer: *Stuff made in the hole isn't the best quality, and the hole can't make big, complicated stuff like hovercars and boards. That's why you have to requisition certain things.*

FAQ 3: *Who designs the stuff that the hole makes?*

Answer: Whoever wants to, and everyone shares their work. It's sort of like making music, fan fiction, or Lolcats and putting them up on the Internet. (In Aya's city, whenever anyone "prints" something that you designed, your face rank goes up.)

FAQ 4: *Why was stuff rationed in Aya's city?*

Answer: Everything takes energy, and the raw materials (the "paper" for the printer) have to be taken from the environment. So as the population rises and non-bubbleheaded people get more creative, the cities all need systems to limit consumption.

Brain Surge

One of the great promises of nanos is their use in medicine. They're small enough to inject into a human body and are "smart" enough to do what we want when they get where they're going.

For example, buckyballs can trap other molecules inside them—the "caged" molecules don't affect anything outside the buckyball. So if you put a toxic medicine inside a buckyball cage, you can safely inject it into a person. Then the buckyball carries the poison around the body until it bumps into a certain kind of target—let's say a cancer cell. The buckyball is programmed to open up when it meets that kind of cell, spilling the toxin in exactly the right place.

The bubblehead nanos act in pretty much the same way, except that they don't attack cancer—they target certain parts of the brain, creating the lesions that make people bubbleheaded.

Scientists have discovered that human brains are divided by function. In other words, there's a part of your brain for seeing, another for hearing, and another for smelling. There are also parts of your brain that are active when you make moral decisions, analyze risks, and laugh at jokes. The parts of the brain that rule creativity haven't been pinned down yet, but once they are, it will be possible to create bubbleheads. (Don't try this at home.)

The Cure

Maddy's cure also uses nanos, tiny machines that are targeted to repair the lesions. The cure actually wasn't so hard to create, because the bubblehead operation was *designed* to be reversed. Even during the Prettytime, firefighters, Rangers, and surgeons were all de-bubbleheaded so that they could do their jobs better.

The problem was that the nanos that Zane took in *Pretties* weren't designed to stop on their own. (He was supposed to take the *other* pill, which Tally took.) Like the grey goo, they just kept eating. This gave him headaches and ultimately brain damage. It's just luck that Maddy cured him in time.

FAQ: *So how did Tally cure* herself?

Answer: *When one part of the brain is damaged, the rest of it tries to take over the missing functions. Here in the real world, people with brain damage rewire themselves all the time without nanos. People sometimes come out of comas after hearing their favorite music, which makes scientists think that stimulation is very important in this process. (Zane was all about stimulation—pulling tricks and trying to remember his ugly days—which he called "staying bubbly.")*

Hungry Nanos

In *Specials*, Tally and Shay break into the Armory, a storehouse of ancient Rusty weapons. One of these is a beaker of silvery nanos with only one purpose: to re-create themselves. They consume anything they touch, spreading like a cancer and finally eating the entire building. This is my version of the "grey goo" scenario discussed above. Of course, I made my nanos silver, because that's more dramatic and intense than boring old gray.

FAQ: *Why didn't the hungry nanos eat the whole world?*

Answer: *My goo was a weapon, not an accidental mutation. So its designers made sure that it wouldn't destroy the entire planet. They programmed it to eat everything except:*

1. The beaker it was stored in. (Duh.)

2. A special "antidote" foam, so that an accidental spill wouldn't doom its makers.

3. Dirt—that's right, plain old dirt. That way, the nanos would stop spreading once an entire building (or city) was gone.

Smart Matter

In *Extras* a new invention has resulted from the mind-rain: smart matter. Smart matter is basically a big pile of general-purpose nanos that can be programmed on the fly. They're sort of like Legos: building blocks that you can use to make anything you want.

A matter hacker broadcasts instructions to smart matter, like sending software to a computer. So you can see why matter hackers are illegal except in the hands of authorized people. If you've just created a cool new building that uses smart matter supports, you don't want someone coming along and turning that matter into, say, liquid. Because that would be bad.

Other Examples

In *Uglies*, David uses nano-glue when they break into Special Circumstances headquarters. These nanos analyze whatever they come into contact with, then become the right sort of glue to stick to it.

In *Pretties*, Tally remembers the Smokies using nanos in their outdoor toilets to break down sewage into fertilizer (and to make the whole business less smelly).

Also in *Pretties*, Maddy explains that pretty teeth are unbreakable, unless you use special "dental nanos" to soften them up.

In *Specials*, Tally has repair nanos stored in her body, so that her muscles and tissues heal very quickly when damaged.

Also in *Specials*, the surge tank is full of "nutrients and nanos to keep her tissues alive while the surgeons were shredding her to pieces." So clearly nanos are a part of every major operation.

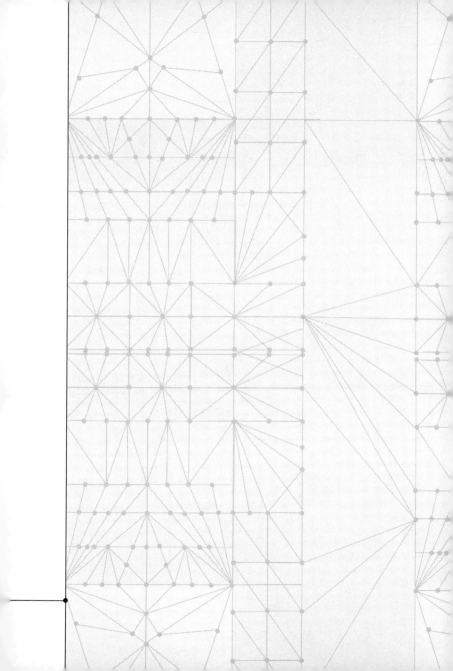

REPUTATION ECONOMIES

No one famous lived in Akira Hall, just loads of face-missing extras, wearing generic designs. A few ego-kickers sat talking into their cams, watched by no one. The average face rank here was six hundred thousand, despair-making and pathetic.

Reputation has always been important

to human beings. We're all hardwired to seek approval from others and to be wary of people who everyone else seems not to like. Some of our great works of fiction—*The Scarlet Letter*, *Dangerous Liaisons*, *School for Scandal*—are about ruined reputations.

Of course, if you're in high school or junior high, I probably don't have to tell *you* about the importance of reputation. But how did I get the idea of having a whole city obsessed with fame and an economy based on reputation?

"DO YOU KNOW PARIS HILTON?"

In this neighborhood, all the buildings moved. They hovered and transformed and did other flabbergasting things, and everyone who lived here was legendarily bored by it all. . . . Hiro lived in the famous part of town.

Sometimes when I'm at bookstores or schools, I get weird questions like, "Do you live in a mansion?" or "Do people recognize you on the street?" or even "Do you know Paris Hilton?" These questions used to surprise me, until I figured out where they were coming from. Fans were trying to figure out how I, their favorite author, fit into the world of fame and celebrity.

After all, fame is important to us. We're surrounded by images of famous people every day. The sales of movies, books, and CDs all are tracked, as if art were one big popularity contest. And it's not like I don't read the bestseller lists myself (especially when I'm on them). Fame does matter, after all—if nothing else, it's nice to know that our favorite moviemakers, musicians, and novelists won't *starve* before they finish their next project.

Of course, most of us run into reputation systems every day. The top-selling novel sits at the front of the bookstore; the number one movie gets more ads on TV; the most-viewed YouTube video is the easiest one to find. In fact, most of you probably started reading *Uglies* because of some sort of reputation system: It was featured in a store, sold in a club, or recommended to you by a friend.

So reputation systems can't be *all* bad, can they?

Note: *I have no mansions, no one recognizes me on the street (unless I'm at a library convention), and I don't know Paris Hilton—but I do know Holly Black, which is way cooler.*

THE WISDOM OF THE INTERNET

The wisdom of the crowd, Aya. If a million people look at a puzzle, chances are that one of them knows the answer. Or maybe ten people each know one piece, and that's enough to put it all together.

—HIRO

In the early Rusty days, information mostly came from authorities: the editors of newspapers, the folks who write encyclopedias, and our wise friends on TV. Back then, bank buildings had giant stone columns to show how serious they were. And when you bought something from a store and it didn't work, you could go back and complain in person.

But these days, thanks to the Internet, we're constantly hearing opinions from people we've never heard of and buying stuff from people we've never met. With credit cards and online banking, our money lives in some weird electronic wonderland we can't even see.

So how do we know who to trust?

Luckily, the Internet happens on computers, which are really good at counting up votes, reviews, and other kinds of ratings. When you're buying a book, looking for a new band, or picking a movie to see, a ranking system will probably pop up to steer you toward the good and away from the bad.

One model of Internet reputation is eBay's. Every time you buy something, you rate the seller. As votes accumulate it's easy to tell who's trustworthy. And the system makes sellers behave, because no one wants to read nasty reviews about themselves. (We authors certainly don't.)

Slashdot.org is an example of an intellectual reputation system. Every post on Slashdot is rated by readers according to how interesting and relevant it is, and higher-ranked posts "bubble up" so that still more people can read them. Smart is rewarded; boring is not.

All of these systems use "the wisdom of the crowd." Instead of one authority, like a newspaper editor, deciding what's true, large numbers of people contribute.

Even anti-spam filters use this concept. Servers that send a lot of spam get a "bad reputation," and their e-mails are scrutinized more closely. So every time you click on JUNK to delete an e-mail, you're part of the "wisdom of the crowd." Just like with fame in Aya's city, you contribute to the process without even noticing you're doing so.

Perhaps these reputation systems are the testing grounds for the economies of the future.

REPUTATION IN *EXTRAS*

"It's just . . . that cam cost me a lot of merits."

"It's a toy. Like face ranks and merits, it doesn't mean anything if you don't let it."

—AYA AND JAI

The key thing about the people in Aya's city is that they use *two* kinds of reputation. You can collect merits, given out by a committee to teachers, doctors, and other nonfamous contributors to society. Or you can worry about your face rank, which everyone has a part in making: Every time someone talks about you, copies the way you dress, hums a song you wrote, or watches your feed, the city interface makes you a little bit more famous— pure crowd logic.

In this way, Aya's city is both old-fashioned and newfangled. They use a panel of authorities, the Good Citizen Committee, *and* the wisdom of the crowd. I figured this would work better than an economy with only one kind of reputation. And it also makes Aya's life more complicated, because she has to do her homework as well as try to become famous.

The debate over expert opinions versus that of the masses actually goes back a long way. (A lot of people argued against democracy at first, because, like, *anybody* could vote.) But how well these two kinds of systems balance each other is a huge topic right now, and will probably remain one throughout your lifetime: Wikipedia or encyclopedia? Blogs or newspapers? Merits or face rank?

The choice is yours.

MISCELLANY

LAST LINES

Notice anything about these three last lines?

"I'm Tally Youngblood. . . . Make me pretty."
—**Tally**

"Face it, Tally-wa, you're Special." —**Shay**

"Be careful with the world, or the next time we meet, it might get ugly." —**Tally**

That's right, you guessed it! The last word in *Uglies* is "pretty," the last word in *Pretties* is "special," and the last word in *Specials* is "ugly." Thanks to all the readers who spotted my little trick. There's no point in us writers putting stuff like that in if you don't notice!

Of course, the last word in *Extras* is "cake," so if I ever write a fifth book, it will have to be called, um, *Cakes*.

I LOVE YOU

The phrase "I love you" appears exactly twice in the trilogy:

Zane says it to Tally in *Pretties*, right before he jumps out of the balloon during their escape. (She never sees him healthy again!)

Tally says it to David at the end of *Specials*, but only as a message from his mom. (Ouch.)

PARTY CRASHING

Be careful, Moggle. We're not wanted here.

—AYA

All four books in the series start the same way, with someone crashing a party. The series starts with ugly Tally crashing a pretty party. Then, in *Pretties*, Croy crashes a pretty party as a Smokie. After they become Special, Tally and friends crash an ugly party. Finally, Aya crashes a tech-head party as an extra/ugly.

What's up with that? Am I condoning party crashing?

Actually, I didn't realize what was going on until the third book, and by then the pattern was set. But I'm glad the party crashing kept happening, because the series is fundamentally about being uncomfortable, both in your own skin and in your society. Having my characters party crash generates those intense feelings of not belonging that drive the books.

Also, the societies that Tally and Aya are growing up in are very much about manners and propriety. Everyone is supposed to know their rightful place in life (or at least their face rank). So the moment someone shows up at the wrong party, the plot thickens.

RADICAL HONESTY

I guess sometimes you have to lie to find the truth.

—FRIZZ

After I had finished writing *Extras*, I learned that there really was a group called Radical Honesty. The founder, Brad Blanton, wrote a book of that name in 1994, which advises its readers to tell the truth every time they open their mouths. Just as *Extras* was coming out, I read an interview with him, and he's not nearly as sweet a guy as Frizz. To read this interview yourself, just Google the phrase "I think you're fat." (Warning: for reasons of radical honesty, the interview contains profanity.)

Of course, the members of real-world Radical Honesty don't have brain surge to enforce their honesty. Part of their philosophy is that you yourself have to make the choice to be honest. With that, I'm sure Frizz would agree.

NEOFOODIES ARE REAL!

A recent movement in food preparation is called "molecular gastronomy." They use scientific equipment and a vast knowledge of chemistry and physics to create weird dishes like the ones in *Extras*. Examples of dishes include popcorn soup, pizza pebbles, sardine sorbet with toast, and salmon poached with licorice. Basically, molecular gastronomists are a cross between chefs and mad scientists, though some people call them "food hackers." Don't be afraid! A lot of the stuff they make is really delicious (and amusingly perplexing). For NeoFoodies in your area, check out WD-50 in New York, Moto and Alinea in Chicago, Le Sanctuaire in San Francisco, and Cafe Atlantico in Washington, D.C.

HIRO RULES

The first sixteen hundred words (about sixty pages) of *Extras* was written from Hiro's perspective rather than Aya's. He was going to be the "Hiro" of the book, because I thought a male perspective on Tally's world would be interesting. But all the cool stuff kept happening to Aya, so I wound up throwing away Hiro's chapters and starting over.

But I did manage to steal a few images here and there, like being "ping-bashed." Here's the original first chapter of *Extras* from Hiro's point of view (and includes some of the original names of the characters):

Hiro woke to the usual ping-bashing: thousands of messages, one night's buildup of tips and scams and invitations. They gabbled at him from attached soundfiles, flickered with videos of surge-monkeys and manga-heads, and bubbled up smiley faces, exclamations, and fluttering hearts.

He lay in bed for a moment, eyes closed, enjoying the rumble of the multitude clamoring for his attention. A good omen for the day.

"Tea, please," he asked the room. "And show my face rank."

As the percolator began to bubble and hiss, Hiro lay there, a nervous tingle building in his stomach. Last night he'd kicked a story—a big story, maybe. He'd stayed up late watching it spread through the feeds, remixed and debated. People were definitely talking.

The question was, were they talking about him?

It was time to find out. Taking a deep breath, he opened his eyes. Meter-high digits flickered on the wallscreen . . . 991.

Hiro stared at the number. Out of a million citizens, his face rank had reached the top thousand. . . .

No wonder he had so many pings in his stack—the story was huge.

Overnight he'd become famous.

He was still staring when his door chime sounded.

"Rez Iyama," said the room.

"Let him in!"

The door slid open and Rez strode through. He glanced at the wallscreen and tried to hide his lip-splitting grin with a deep bow.

"Meditating, Hiro-chan? Or are you too famous to get out of bed?"

Hiro sat up and dragged on a hoverball sweatshirt, smiling himself. Rez joking about it made his rank suddenly seem real. "Guess I stayed up late."

"Waste of beauty sleep," Rez said. "Your face didn't move much last night. But when the crumblies started waking up, you went legendary."

"Of course!" Hiro rolled his eyes at his own stupidity.

He'd kicked the story late at night, to let it build with feed-junkies and tech-heads. But the story was really about crumblies. . . .

A few days before, Hiro had received a random ping laying out a weird conspiracy theory: Doctors secretly knew how to keep people alive forever. He'd followed up and discovered a new clique of crumbly surge-monkeys. Unlike normal surgery addicts, they didn't care about beauty or freaky body mods—only life extension. Liver refits every six months, new cloned hearts once a year.

The only reason anyone died of old age, they were convinced, was to keep the population steady. It was just like the brain lesions back in the Prettytime: The doctors were hiding the truth.

So the crumblies were planning to sue the city . . . for immortality.

They were crazy, probably, but that never stopped a good story. All night the debate had been kicking through the city interface. Was immortality a bogus idea? Could your brain stay bubbly forever? And if no one died, where on earth would you put everybody?

All that talk had pushed Hiro's rank to its best spot ever. Out of a million citizens, 991 was awesome face.

"I guess we can't hang out anymore." Rez sighed. "Now that you're top thousand."

Hiro laughed. Before this morning's craziness, Rez had been a lot more famous than him, with a face rank that usually broke ten thousand. He was a tech-kicker, his feed packed with hardware designs and city interface mods. Most extras didn't care about Rez's tricks, but he was legendary to the people who mattered.

The wallscreen flickered with a rankings update, and they both turned to watch. Hiro had lost face, dropping to 997.

"Huh," he said. "Immortality sure got old fast."

"That's what you get for sleeping late," Rez said. "You'll be back to six figures in no time. Do I smell tea?"

Rolling out of bed, Hiro put two mugs under the percolator. Green tea swirled from the spigots, filling the room with the smell of cut grass and caffeine.

"I liked your last image," Rez said. "The cities growing. Scary."

"Yeah, can you imagine?" Hiro shuddered. He'd used satellite pictures from the Rusty era: billions of extras crowding the planet, most living in total obscurity. If everyone lived forever, how long would it take humanity to fill up the planet again?

He pulled his mug from under the percolator and took a swig.

"Mmph!" The still-boiling tea burned its way

across his lips and tongue. He forced himself to swallow, and the liquid seared his throat. "Ouch!"

"Do you need medical attention?" asked the room.

"No!" He angrily blew on the tea.

"Nice one, Hiro-chan." Rez grinned, inhaling the scent from his mug. "Maybe you should set your room to 'bubblehead.'"

Hiro snorted. Back in the Prettytime, the hole in the wall wouldn't give you anything tongue-scalding. True, the tea was much better this way, but only if you remembered not to burn yourself.

Freedom had some annoying features.

"Should we check the competition?" Hiro asked.

Rez nodded, then told the room, "Top twelve."

The wallscreen split into a dozen panels: the most popular kickers in Yokohama. Hiro took a cautious sip of his tea. It was the usual bunch; no new faces had hit the top twelve in a month.

The familiar voices washed over Hiro like a conversation with old friends, soothing his burn-addled nerves. The city's big faces weren't just idols, they were companions. Sometimes it felt like he knew them better than he did himself.

He wondered if after last night's story, any of them actually knew his name in return. But *none of them was kicking immortality.*

In the upper right corner, Frizz Motsui had discovered yet another new religion. Some pre-Rusty-history clique had averaged the world's great spiritual books with an AI, then programmed it to spit out godlike decrees. For some reason, the software had told them not to eat pigs.

But who would do that in the first place?

"Pig-eating!" Rez giggled. "They seriously need to debug that code."

"Gods are so last year," Hiro said.

Resurrecting old religions had been kicked right after the mind-rain, when everyone was still trying to figure out what all the new freedoms meant. But these days so many other things had been rediscovered—karate and family reunions and manga and the cherry blossom festival—that most people were too busy to try to impress invisible superheroes.

"What's the Nameless One doing?" Rez said, switching the sound to another feed.

The Nameless One was Yosh Banana—the most brain-missing kicker in Yokohama. Hiro and Rez had suffered through littlie school with Yosh, and ten years later the guy was still an inescapable bully, always picking on some new clique. He seemed to think the mind-rain was a bad thing, just because other people's obsessions could seem so weird these days.

This morning he was yammering about

ghastly pet-breeding experiments. A dog appeared, dyed pink and sprouting weird tufts of fur.

"It's just a poodle, you moron!" Rez shouted, tossing a pillow at the wallscreen.

"Even the Rusties had those," Hiro said. One eye-kicking pet was hardly the first step on the path back to fur coats—or eating pigs, for that matter.

"Kill that feed," Rex told the room. Every second they spent watching Yosh boosted his already overstuffed ranking. Even mentioning someone's name while the city interface could hear you—which was always—went into the face stats. In the reputation economy, the best way to hurt someone was to ignore them.

Rez brought up the rankings, checking which stories were making their kickers more famous. The AI religion was a flop—Frizz had lost face all morning. But the weird-looking dog was working, sending the Nameless One all the way up to 275.

"Depressing," Rez pronounced. Then he smiled. "Shall we check in on Ama-chan?"

Hiro sighed. He needed to get to work on the stack of pings, but he couldn't resist the second-most-famous person in Yokohama.

"Okay, maybe for a minute."

The screens flipped to twelve new feeds, all dedicated to Ama Love.

She was having a breakfast of plum sandwiches and chatting with her surged-up friends about the parties they'd dropped in on last night. From a dozen angles, her huge eyes seemed to gaze straight at Hiro—somehow the hundreds of paparazzi cams hovering in the background didn't spoil the intimacy. Crowded ranks of icons showed the other feeds covering her, with the choice of adoring, mocking, and outright obsessed streams of commentary.

It was the same chatter as every morning, and Hiro had work to do, but it wasn't easy tearing himself away. He hated getting stuck in feeds—it was better to be watched instead—but there was something about Ama's legendary face that made him shiver. All that beauty and not one cut of surge.

The only natural-born pretty in a generation.

"Hey, did you catch that?" Rez said. "They're talking about the party!"

"What party?" Hiro tried to focus through Ama's dazzling glow.

"The party. The Thousand Faces is in three weeks." Rez punched Hiro's shoulder. "Awesome timing for you!"

"No way," Hiro murmured. One night every year, Ama invited the thousand most-famous Yokohamans to her mansion. The event filled every feed in the city, and everyone watched—even those who lied and said they didn't.

If he could keep his ranking up, Hiro Torrent might actually be one of the Thousand Faces this year.

He glanced out the window—the sky was bright, the heavy clouds like burnished gray metal. Even light, no shadows; a perfect day for hovercams.

"Rez, it's time I got kicking."

"You're right." Rez stood up, bowing low at the door. "Good luck today, Hiro-chan."

"Thanks. I'll need it." Rule number one of fame: Follow up a big kick with an even bigger one.

Hiro cleared his wallscreen, feeling the usual tug of melancholy as Ama's face disappeared. But he had work to do: thousands of pings to explore. Humanity was free now, with wild new forms of insanity and brilliance to invent. Millions of extras were out there, begging to be noticed.

There was a big story in the pile—he could feel it. Something bigger than poodles, plum sandwiches, and rumors of immortality.

All Hiro had to do was track it down.

FICTIONAL REPUTATION SYSTEMS

Thanks to all the ranking systems on the Internet, lots of science fiction writers have been asking if reputation will ever replace money. Here's a couple of books that I borrowed while working on *Extras*. (Remember: It's okay to steal ideas, as long as you mention where they came from!)

In Cory Doctorow's 2003 novel *Down and Out in the Magic Kingdom*, a currency called "whuffie" works sort of like merits in Aya's city. Every time you do something good for the community (from baking cookies to fixing the problem of air pollution), you get whuffie. You lose whuffie when you do something bad, like playing your music too loud and keeping everyone awake.

In Iain M. Banks's 2004 novel *The Algebraist*, a fame/reputation system uses a currency called "kudos," from the Greek word for praise. It's a bit more like face rank than merits. In Charles Stross's *Accelerando*, the hero makes a career of giving away ideas and living off only his reputation. And in Bruce Sterling's *Distraction*, a motorcycle gang determines its members' status by online voting. (Hah!)

CUTTING

*Right. You're so special no one can touch you. . . . You're
so special you have to cut yourself just to feel anything.*

—ZANE

A lot of readers have asked about the cutting in the
books. Was I thinking about the cutting that some
teenagers do in our modern-day world? Well, yes.
But I was also thinking about the way cutting and
plastic surgery fit together in our society.

Surgery also involves slicing flesh, after all,
and both cutting and cosmetic surgery stem from
not feeling right in your own body. Society accepts
face-lifts and nose jobs, while, for obvious reasons,
cutting is considered an illness. But in a way they're
two sides of the same coin.

It didn't make sense to me for Tally's world to have
one and not the other. The books are partly about how
our beliefs get expressed through our bodies—flash
tattoos for Crims, beauty for bubbleheads, and super-
strength for Specials. The media-obsessed people
in Aya's city all have eyescreens, and the Extras, who
want to live in space, have genuinely alien bodies. So it
seemed kind of lame not to include the dark side of this
phenomenon: the way that people's desperate need to
feel something involves harm to themselves.

After all, to help people who cut themselves, we have to at least try to understand what's going on inside their heads. I've gotten a lot of e-mail from teens who injure themselves, actually. A few found those parts of the books too intense and skipped right past them. But most said that I'd captured some aspect of their experience in a way that helped them.

Seeing a part of your own life in a book, especially one set in a faraway time and place, can give you perspective. I hope that the Uglies series has helped a few of you resolve issues, whether with cutting or looks or your own struggles against the Dr. Cables of this world.

GLOSSARY

Bogus is used by pretties to mean anything bad or broken. It's the opposite of "bubbly." I stole "bogus" from Evelyn Waugh's *Vile Bodies*, about a rich, party-loving social group in the 1920s. The "pretty young things" in Waugh's novel also use "shaming" and "nervous-making," so I stole those too.

Bubbleheads is a dismissive term for pretties. Originally, only Specials used this word to show their superiority to the pretty-minded. But after the mind-rain, everyone began to use it for citizens who chose *not* to reverse the mental effects of the operation.

Bubbly means a lot of things to pretties: the champagne they drink, the way they act at parties, and how they feel when they like someone. Anything stimulating is bubbly. It's a lazy way to talk, but the pretties are lazy-brains, so I thought it made sense for their world to fall into two simple categories (see **bogus**). Of course, when Tally and Zane start to be cured, they use "bubbly" as their secret code for "thinking clearly." (In a way, they're flipping the meaning of the word to its opposite.)

Bungee jackets are safety devices for building evacuation. (See "Gadgets and Inventions.")

Crash bracelets are hoverboard safety equipment. (See "Hoverboard Manual.")

Crims are Zane's clique, named after Australian slang for "criminals." (See "Cliques.")

Crumblies is slang for late pretties. Uglies also tend to call their parents "crumblies," even if they're only middle pretties. In our world, "crumbly" is British slang for an older person. (See "Life Phases in the Prettytime.")

Crumblyville is where late pretties live, tending to their gardens and waiting out their life-extension treatments. (See "Maps.")

The cure is the term for the unauthorized de-bubbleheading nanos invented by Maddy. Easy to produce and fast-acting, the cure was widely distributed and caused the mind-rain and the end of the Prettytime.

Cutters See "Cliques."

Diego is a city where the government was never as controlling as in other cities. Teachers and other care-givers were not given the bubblehead operation, which encouraged independent thinking in all levels of society. For this reason, the mind-rain started here, though it was first called the "New System."

The Diego War was a conflict between Tally's city and Diego, and was the first organized warfare in a hundred years. It was caused by Dr. Cable, who disapproved of Diego's New System, which allowed citizens to reverse the effects of the bubblehead operation if they wanted. Diego also harbored runaways from other cities. (See "History #5: The Diego War.")

Expansion is a general term for the population and construction explosion caused by the mind-rain. With the constraints of the Prettytime lifted, no one knows how far the cities will expand into the wild.

Extras is a slang term in Aya's city for people who aren't famous. It also is a secret clique, Extraterrestrials, dedicated to space colonization. (See "Cliques.")

Eyescreens are surgical implants that allow the user to see the city interface at all times. (See "Gadgets and Inventions.")

Face rank is a measure of all attention paid to a person detected by the city interface. In Aya's city, mentioning people's name, watching their feed, and any use of their intellectual output (designs, music, text) increases their face rank.

Fashion-missing means uncool, out of fashion, or someone who simply doesn't seem to care. Also "face-missing."

Feeds are a combination of what we call television and the Internet—everything from personal sites to the official government news services. In Aya's city, everyone gets their own feed when they turn twelve. This way everyone who's not a littlie has an equal chance to become famous.

Flash tattoos are subcutaneous digital displays. In other words, tattoos that move, usually triggered by heartbeat or other biological functions. The first were used to warn diabetics of blood sugar shifts, but eventually they became a fashion item, and were especially popular with Crims and Cutters.

Hoverboards are an old science fiction idea: a magnetically levitating surface halfway in size between a surfboard and a skateboard. (See "Hoverboard Manual" and "Science #2: Magnetic Levitation.")

Hovercams are semiautonomous cameras with hover-lifters. They were originally developed for gathering news and covering sports, but in Aya's city, where everyone has their own feed, they became a common personal accessory.

Icy is what the Cutters say instead of bubbly. Specials are much scarier than pretties, so I wanted them to use a word that sounded cold and sharp instead of frothy and fun.

Kickers get famous by publicizing things that other people do. Sort of a cross between journalists and bloggers.

Late pretties are people old enough to have started to get life-extension treatments. Also known as **crumblies**. (See "Life Phases in the Prettytime.")

Lifter rigs are the superconducting magnets found in all hovering devices. (See "Science #2: Magnetic Levitation.")

Littlies are anyone under the age of twelve. Littlies still live with their parents and are cute and small enough not to be called uglies. This is one of many slang words I stole from Australia, where it means younger kids, like toddlers. (See "Life Phases in the Prettytime.")

Manga-heads are people in Aya's city who get surge to look like manga characters. (See "Cliques.")

Merits are what the council of Aya's city give to doctors, teachers, and other workers who won't ever get famous and yet are very important to society. Like face rank, merits can be acquired by everyone to exchange for goods and housing. The main difference is that merits, like money, run out, and you have to make more. Face rank lasts as long as you can stay famous.

Milli-Helen is exactly the right amount of beauty to launch one ship. This is Zane's joking reference to Helen of Troy, a pre-Rusty natural pretty whose beauty started the legendary war between Greece and Troy. (Her face was said to have "launched a thousand ships," meaning the Greek invasion force.) I stole this joke from Ben Schott of *Schott's Original Miscellany*.

Mind-rain is the common term for the spread across the globe of the cure for bubbleheadedness, which brought about a global period of creativity and new inventions. (See "History #6: The Mind-Rain and the Extras.")

Nanos are invisibly small machines. (See "Science #3: Nanos.")

New pretties are people who have recently had the operation. The bubblehead effect is so strong that they really can't do much but party, so they all live together in New Pretty Town. (See "Life Phases in the Prettytime.")

New Pretty Town is where new pretties live (duh). In Tally's city, it was located on an island in the middle of town. The river kept those nasty uglies out of the pleasure gardens. (See "Maps.")

New System When Maddy's cure reached Diego, the city government began to reassess the operation. At first, being bubbleheaded became optional, and then *all* forms of control over the operation were dropped. Resistance to the New System was the cause of the Diego War.

Pings are messages carried by the city interface, the ever-present system of communication and control. Pings carry any kind of data you want, a combination of e-mail, voice mail, and text-messaging. The city AI listens in on pings, and flags any it deems suspicious for the authorities. I stole this term from corporate slang for an e-mail that reminds you to do something, as in, "She didn't send me that budget on time, so I pinged her about it."

Position-finder See "Gadgets and Inventions."

Pre-Rusties are the people who lived before industrialization. Maybe they didn't have hoverboards, but at least their primitive cultures didn't destroy Earth.

Pretties are people who have had the operation. In the Italian translation of *Uglies*, pretties were called *perfetti*, which literally means "perfects." I thought that was cool. (See "Life Phases in the Prettytime.")

The Pretty Committee is the common name for the Committee for Morphological Standards. (See "History #2: The Rise of the Cities and the Pretty Committee.")

Prettytime is the long period when the bubblehead operation kept control of humanity's appetites, cutting down on pollution, conflict, and population growth. Much of human culture stopped progressing during this era, which was marked by strong central governments and peace among the cities.

Reputation Bombers are a clique in Aya's city who pump up their face ranks through cheating. I took the term from "Google bombing," a set of techniques for boosting the Google rank of a search phrase for propaganda purposes. (In other words, trying to make your hotel the first one to appear when the word "hotel" is searched on Google.)

Reputation Economy See "Reputation Economies."

Rusties are the oil-dependent culture that destroyed itself three hundred years before the books take place. (They are, of course, us.) Everyone calls them Rusties because that's all that's left of our culture: rust-covered ruins. (See "History #1: The Rusty Crash.")

Smart matter See "Science #3: Nanos."

The Smoke is where the rebel Smokies live. It's called that because the runaways burn wood for heat, which city pretties would never do. In the early industrial age, London was called "The Smoke," because its factory smokestacks filled the sky with gray clouds. A few people still use the nickname, which I've always liked.

Smokies are a group of rebels and runaways started by Maddy and Az, two surgeons who uncovered the bubblehead effect. They lived in a rustic mountain camp, using a combination of traditional and high technologies. They recruited runaway uglies from the cities, which ultimately led to their being tracked down and recaptured by Special Circumstances.

Sneak suits are adaptive camouflage devices used by Special Circumstances. (See "Gadgets and Inventions.")

SpagBol is Australian slang for spaghetti Bolognese. (Australians avoid saying long words if they can help it.) Back when she was a littlie, my sister-in-law ate almost nothing but spaghetti Bolognese for six years. I thought that was funny, so I had Tally undergo a similar experience: SpagBol, SpagBol, SpagBol . . .

Specials are members of Special Circumstances, the secret branch of the city government that has replaced the military and intelligence services. They have their own kind of surgery that makes them "cruel pretties," beautiful but scary. In his utopian Culture series, Scottish novelist Iain Banks uses the term "Special Circumstances" for the government's secret enforcers. So I stole it. (See "History #3: Special Circumstances and the Smoke.")

Suburbs are where middle pretties and their littlies live. (See "Maps.")

Surge is short for surgery. The fact that pretties find the word "surgery" too long to say suggests how often they say it—we always shorten the words that we use most often in our culture.

Surge-monkeys are people who take cosmetic surgery to extremes, often to achieve fame or notoriety.

The Thousand Faces Party is an annual bash at Nana Love's residence in Aya's city to which the thousand most-famous citizens are invited. (Also called the "Top Tenth Party," because one thousand is roughly a tenth of a percent of the population.)

Tricks are very important in the world of Uglies. The city is very tightly controlled, so any time uglies can trick the authorities, they score a small victory. That's why I use "tricking" in the way we use "hacking"—not fooling just one person, but undermining a whole system.

Uglies are between the ages of twelve and sixteen. Not cute enough to be littlies, not old enough to get the operation. (See "Life Phases in the Prettytime.")

Uglyville is where the uglies live in dormitories, wearing uniforms and insulting one another. A soul-destroying place designed to make you yearn for New Pretty Town. (See "Maps.")

Wardens are the city's police force. Because of the compliant population, they usually deal with simple issues like trespassing and truancy. Miscreant uglies are their main concern.

A NOTE TO THE READER ABOUT
THE COVERS

From the Editor

The photograph on the cover of this book was actually an outtake from the *Uglies* photo shoot. For an important book, sometimes several different versions are shot. We chose the (real) cover for *Uglies* because it is so seductive, and evocative of the wild. While the image featured on the cover of *Bogus to Bubbly* didn't make the final cut for *Uglies*, it's perfect for an insider's guide.

Other fun facts about the covers in the series? If you look carefully in Tally's eyes on *Uglies*, you can see the reflection of the photographer. And on *Extras*, the design for Aya's eyescreen was inspired by a 1980s video game, The Last Starfighter. When we started, little did we know that eyes would become such an important element on the covers.

Look for the first book in
Scott Westerfeld's new series:

LEVIATHAN

Coming in 2009 from Simon Pulse

CHAPTER ONE

T he Austrian horses glinted in the moonlight, their riders standing tall in the saddle, swords raised. Behind them two ranks of diescl-powered walking machines stood ready to fire, cannons aimed over the heads of the cavalry. A zeppelin scouted no-man's-land at the center of the battlefield, its metal skin sparkling.

The French infantry crouched behind their fortifications—a letter opener, an ink jar, and a line of fountain pens—knowing they stood no chance against the might of the Austro-Hungarian Empire. But a row of Darwinist monsters loomed behind them, ready to devour any who dared retreat.

The attack had almost begun when Prince Aleksandar thought he heard someone outside his door.

He took a guilty step toward his bed—then froze in place, listening hard. Trees stirred in a soft breeze outside, but otherwise the night was silent. Mother and Father were in Sarajevo, after all, and the servants wouldn't dare disturb his sleep.

Alek turned back to his desk and began to move the cavalry forward, grinning as the battle neared its climax. The walkers had completed their bombardment, and it was time for the tin horses to finish off the woefully outnumbered French. It had taken all night to set up the attack, using an imperial tactics manual borrowed from Father's study.

It seemed only fair that Alek have some fun while his parents were gone. He'd begged to be taken along, to see the mustered ranks of soldiers striding past in real life, to feel the rumble of massed fighting machines through the soles of his boots.

It was Mother, of course, who had forbidden it—his studies were more important than "parades," as she called them. She didn't seem to understand that military maneuvers had more to teach him than musty old tutors and their books. One day soon Alek might be piloting one of those machines.

War was coming, after all. Everyone said so.

The last cavalry unit had just crashed into the French lines when the soft sound came from the hallway again: jingling.

Alek turned, peering at the gap beneath his bedchamber's double doors. Shadows shifted along the sliver of moonlight, and he heard the hiss of whispers.

Someone was right outside.

Silent in bare feet, he swiftly crossed the cold marble floor, sliding into bed just as the door creaked open. Alek narrowed his eyes to slits, wondering which of the servants was checking up on him, already planning how to take his revenge.

Moonlight spilled into the room, making the tin soldiers on his desk glitter. A figure slipped inside, graceful and dead silent. It paused, staring at Alek for a moment, then crept toward his dresser. He heard the wooden rasp of a drawer sliding open.

Alek's heart raced. None of his servants would dare steal from him!

The intruder might be worse than a thief, though. His father's warnings echoed in his ears. . . .

You have had enemies from the day you were born.

A bell cord hung next to his bed, but his parents' rooms were empty. With Father and his bodyguard in Sarajevo, the closest sentries were quartered at the other end of the trophy hall, fifty long meters away.

Alek slid one hand under his pillow until his fingers felt the cold steel of a hunting knife. He lay there holding his breath, grasping the handle tighter, repeating to himself his father's other watchword. . . .

Surprise is more valuable than strength.

Another figure came through the door then, boots clomping, a piloting jacket's metal clips and clasps jingling. The figure tromped straight toward his bed.

"Young Master! Wake up!"

Alek let go of the knife, expelling a sigh of relief. It was just old Otto Klopp, his master of mechaniks.

The other figure emerged from the shadows behind Otto.

"The young prince has been awake all along," Wildcount Volger's low voice said. "A bit of advice, Your Highness? When pretending to be asleep, it is advisable not to hold one's breath."

Alek sat up and scowled. His fencing master had an annoying knack for seeing through deception.

"What's the meaning of sneaking into my room?"

"You're to come with us, Young Master," Otto mumbled, studying the marble floor. "The archduke's orders."

"My father? He's back already?"

"He left instructions," Count Volger said with the same infuriating tone he used during fencing lessons. He tossed a pair of Alek's trousers and a piloting jacket onto the bed.

Alek stared at them, half outraged and half confused.

"Like young Mozart," Volger said softly.

"Mozart?"

"The archduke's stories," Otto said, "about how genius is cultivated."

Alek frowned, remembering Father's peculiar tales about the

great composer's upbringing. Mozart's tutors would wake him in the middle of the night, when his mind was raw and defenseless, and thrust musical lessons upon him. It all sounded rather disrespectful to Alek.

He reached for the trousers. "You're going to make me compose a fugue?"

"Very amusing, Your Highness," Count Volger said. "But please make haste."

"We have a walker waiting behind the stables, Young Master." Otto's worried face made an attempt at a smile. "You're to take the helm."

"A walker?" Alek's eyes widened. Piloting was one part of his studies he'd gladly get out of bed for. He slipped quickly into the clothes.

"Yes, your first night lesson!" Otto whispered, handing Alek his boots.

Alek pulled them on and stood, crossing the room to fetch his favorite driving gloves, his footsteps echoing on the marble.

"Quietly now." Count Volger stood by the chamber doors. He cracked them open and peered out into the hall.

"We're to sneak out, Your Highness!" Otto whispered. "Good fun, this lesson! Just like young Mozart!"

The three of them crept down the trophy hall, Master Klopp still clomping, Volger gliding along in silence. Paintings of Alek's ancestors, the family who had ruled Austria for six hundred years, stared down with unreadable expressions. The antlers of his father's hunting trophies cast tangled shadows, like a moonlit forest. Every footstep was magnified by the empty stillness of the castle, and questions echoed in Alek's mind.

Wasn't it dangerous piloting a walker at night? And why was his fencing master coming along? Volger preferred swords and horses over soulless mechaniks, and had little tolerance for commoners like old Otto. Master Klopp had been hired for his piloting skills, not his family name.

"Otto . . . ?" Alek began.

"Quiet, boy!" the wildcount hissed.

Anger flashed inside Alek, and a curse almost burst from his mouth, even if it would ruin their stupid game of sneaking out.

It was always like this. To the servants he might be "the young archduke," but nobles like Volger never let Alek forget his position. Thanks to his mother's blood, he wasn't fit to inherit royal lands and titles. His father might be heir to an empire of fifty million souls, but Alek was heir to nothing.

Volger himself was only a wildcount—no farmlands to his name, just a bit of forest—but even he could feel superior to the son of a lady-in-waiting.

But Alek managed to stay quiet, letting his anger cool as they stole through the vast and darkened banquet kitchens. The years of insults had taught him how to bite his tongue, and disrespect was easier to swallow with the prospect of piloting ahead.

One day he would have his revenge, Father had promised. The marriage contract would be changed somehow, and Alek's blood made royal.

Even if it meant defying the emperor himself.

CHAPTER TWO

By the time they reached the stables, Alek's only concern was tripping in the darkness. The moon was less than half full, and the estate's hunting forests stretched like a black sea across the valley. At this hour even the lights of Prague had died out to a mere inkling.

When Alek saw the walker, a soft cry escaped his lips.

Crouching there, it stood taller than the stable's roof, its two metal feet sunk deep into the soil of the riding paddock. It looked like one of the Darwinists' monsters skulking in the darkness.

This wasn't some training machine—it was a real engine of war, a Cyklop Stormwalker. A cannon was mounted in its belly, and the stubby noses of two Spandau machine guns sprouted from its head, which was as big and square as a smokehouse.

Before tonight, Alek had only piloted unarmed runabouts and four-legged training corvettes. Even with his sixteenth birthday almost here, Mother insisted that he was too young for war machines.

"I'm supposed to pilot that?" Alek heard his own voice break. "My old runabout wouldn't come up to its knee!"

Otto Klopp's gloved hand patted his shoulder heavily. "Don't worry, Young Mozart. I'll be at your side."

Count Volger called up to the machine, and its engines rumbled to life, the ground trembling under Alek's feet. Moonlight shivered from wet leaves caught in the camouflage nets hung over the Stormwalker, and the mutter of nervous horses filtered from the stable. The chains of the walker's land anchors began to wind, pulling them up from the ground.

The belly hatch swung open and a chain ladder tumbled out, unrolling as it fell. Count Volger stilled its swinging, then planted a boot on the lowermost metal rung to hold it steady.

"Young Master, if you please."

Alek stared up at the machine. This already outlandish night was suddenly much stranger. He tried to imagine guiding this monster through the darkness, crushing trees, buildings, and anything else unlucky enough to be in his path.

Otto Klopp leaned closer. "Your father the archduke has thrown us a challenge, me and you. He wants you ready to pilot any machine in the empire, even in the middle of the night."

Alek swallowed. Father always said that with war on the horizon, everyone in the household had to be prepared. And it made sense to begin training while Mother was away. If Alek came out of a walker crash covered with bruises, the worst might have faded before the princess Sophie returned.

But still Alek hesitated. The hatchway of the rumbling machine looked like the jaws of some giant predator bending down to take a bite.

"Of course, we cannot compel you, Your Serene Highness," Count Volger said, amusement in his voice. "We can always explain to your father that you felt intimidated."

"I'm not scared." Alek grabbed the ladder, hoisting himself into the air. The saw-toothed metal rungs gripped his gloves, and Volger held the ladder steady as Alek climbed past the razor-sharp antiboarding spikes arrayed along the Cyklop's belly. He crawled into the machine's dark maw, the smell of kerosene and sweat filling his nose, the engines' rhythm trembling in his bones.

"Welcome aboard, Your Highness," a voice said. Two silhouettes waited in the cabin, steel helmets glimmering. A

Stormwalker carried a crew of six, Alek recalled; this wasn't some little two-man runabout. He almost forgot to return their salutes.

Count Volger was close behind him on the ladder, and soon all three of them were inside, the hatch firmly shut. Alek climbed into the pilot's seat, strapping himself in.

He placed his hands on the control saunters, feeling the machine's awesome power trembling in his fingers.

Klopp took the commander's chair and called, "Vision at full!"

The two crewmen cranked the viewport open as wide as it would go. Moonlight spilled into the Stormwalker's cabin, and Alek's gaze fell across a hundred switches and levers.

The four-legged corvette he'd piloted last month had only needed control saunters, a fuel gauge, and a compass. But now uncountable needles were arrayed before him, shivering like nervous whiskers.

What were they all for?

He pulled his eyes from the controls and stared through the viewport. The distance to the ground gave him a queasy feeling, like peering down from a hayloft with thoughts of jumping.

The edge of the forest loomed only twenty meters away. Did they really expect him to pilot this machine for his very first time through those dense trees and tangled roots . . . at night?

"At your pleasure, Young Master," Volger said, sounding bored already.

Alek set his jaw, resolving not to provide the man with any more amusement. He eased the saunters forward, and the huge Daimler engines changed pitch as steel gears bit, grinding into motion.

The Cyklop rose from its crouch slowly, the ground slipping still farther away. Alek could see across the treetops now, all the way to shimmering Prague.

He pulled the left saunter back and pushed the right forward. The machine lumbered into motion with an inhumanly large step, pressing him back into the pilot's seat.

The right pedal rose a little as the walker's foot hit soft ground, nudging Alek's boot. He twisted at the saunters, transferring weight from one foot to the other. The cabin swayed like a tree house in a high wind, lurching back and forth with each giant step. A chorus of hissing came from the engines below, gauges dancing as the Stormwalker's pneumatic joints strained against its weight.

"Good . . . excellent," Otto muttered from the commander's seat. "Watch your knee pressure, though."

Alek dared a glance down at the controls, but had no idea what Master Klopp was talking about. Knee pressure? How could anyone keep track of all those needles without driving the whole contraption into a tree?

"Better," the man said a few steps later. Alek nodded dumbly, overjoyed that he hadn't tipped them over yet.

But already the forest was looming up, filling the wide-open viewport with a dark tangle of shapes. The first glistening branches swept past, thwacking at the viewport, spattering Alek with cold showers of dew.

"Shouldn't we spark up the running lights?" he asked.

Klopp shook his head. "The dark is better. Remember, Young Master? As if we don't want to be spotted."

"Revolting way to travel," Volger muttered, and Alek

wondered again why the man was here. Was there to be a fencing lesson after this? What sort of warrior-Mozart was his father trying to make him into?

The shriek of grinding gears filled the cabin. The left pedal snapped up against his foot, and the whole machine tipped ominously forward.

"You're caught, Young Master!" Otto said, hands ready to snatch the saunters away.

"I know!" Alek cried, twisting at the controls. He slammed the machine's right foot down midstride, its knee joint spitting air like a train whistle. The Stormwalker wavered uncertainly for a moment, drunkenly threatening to fall. But long seconds later Alek felt the machine's weight settle into the moss and dirt. It was balanced with one foot stretching back, like a fencer posing after a lunge.

He pushed on both saunters, the left leg pulling at whatever had entangled it, the right straining forward. The Daimler engines groaned, and a hissing rose up around them. Finally a shudder passed through the cabin, along with the satisfying sound of roots tearing from the ground; the Stormwalker rose up. It stood high for a moment, like a chicken on one leg, then stepped forward again.

Alek's shaking hands guided the walker through its next few strides.

"Well done, Young Master!" Otto cried. He clapped his hands once.

"Thank you, Klopp," Alek said in a dry voice, feeling sweat trickle down his face. His hands clenched the saunters tight, but the machine was walking smoothly again.

Gradually he forgot that he was at the controls, and he felt the steps as if they were his own. The sway of the cabin settled into his body, the hissing rhythms of gears and pneumatics not so different from his runabout's, only louder and deeper. Alek had even begun to see patterns in the flickering needles of the control panel—a few leaped into the red with every footfall, easing back as the Cyklop straightened. Knee pressure, indeed.

But the sheer power of the machine kept him anxious. Heat from the engines built in the cabin, the night air blowing in like cold fingers. Alek tried to imagine what piloting would be like in battle, the viewport squinting against flying bullets and shrapnel.

Finally the pine branches cleared before them, and Klopp said, "Turn here and we'll have better footing, Young Master."

"Isn't this one of Mother's riding paths?" Alek said. "She'll have my hide if we track it up!" Whenever one of Princess Sophie's horses stumbled on a walker footprint, Master Klopp, Alek, and even Father felt her wrath for days.

But he eased back on the throttle, grateful for a moment of rest, bringing the Stormwalker to a halt on the trail. Inside his piloting jacket, Alek was soaked with sweat.

"Disagreeable in every way, Your Highness," Volger said. "But necessary if we're to make good time tonight."

Alek turned to Otto Klopp and frowned. "Make good time? But this is just practice. We're not going anywhere, are we?"

Klopp didn't answer, his eyes glancing up at the count. Alek pulled his hands from the saunters and swiveled the pilot's chair around.

"Volger, what's going on?"

The count and the two crewmen stared down at him in silence, and Alek felt suddenly very alone out here in the darkness.

His mind began to replay his father's warnings: how some nobles believed that Aleksandar's muddled lineage threatened the empire, and how one day the insults might turn into something worse. . . .

But these men couldn't be traitors. Wildcount Volger had held a sword to his throat a thousand times in fencing practice, and his master of mechaniks? Unthinkable.

"What do you mean, Otto? Explain this at once."

"You're to come with us, Your Highness," Klopp said softly.

"We have to get as far away from Prague as possible," Count Volger said. "Your father's orders."

"But my father isn't even . . ." Alek gritted his teeth and swore. What a fool he'd been, tempted into the forest with tales of Mozart and midnight piloting, like luring a child with candy. The whole household was asleep, his parents away in Sarajevo.

Alek's arms still trembled from fighting to keep the Storm-walker upright, and strapped into the pilot's chair he could hardly draw his knife—he closed his eyes—even if he hadn't left it back in his room, under the pillow.

"The archduke left us instructions," Count Volger said.

"You're lying!" Alek shouted.

"I wish we were, Young Master." Volger reached into his riding jacket.

A surge of white-hot anger swept into Alek, cutting through his despair. These traitors might be bigger and stronger, but they weren't taking him without a fight!

His hands shot to the unfamiliar controls, searching for the distress whistle's cord. They couldn't be far from home yet; surely someone would hear the Cyklop's shriek!

The two crewmen jumped into motion, grabbing his arms. Volger swept a flask from his jacket and forced its open mouth against Alek's face. A sweet smell filled the cabin, sending his mind spinning. He tried not to breathe, struggling against the larger men all around him.

Then his fingers found the distress cord and pulled. . . .

But Master Klopp's hands were already at the controls, spilling the Stormwalker's pneumatic pressure. The whistle only let out a miserable descending wail, like a tea kettle pulled from the fire.

Alek still struggled, holding his breath for what felt like minutes, but finally his lungs rebelled. He scooped in a ragged breath, the sharp scent of chemicals filling his head. . . .

A cascade of bright spots fell across the instruments, and a weight seemed to lift from Alek's shoulders. He felt as though he were floating free of the men's grasp, free of the seat straps—free of gravity, even.

"My father will have your heads," he managed to croak.

"Alas not, Your Highness," Count Volger said. "Your parents are both dead, murdered last night in Sarajevo."

Alek tried to laugh at this absurd statement, but the world twisted sideways under him, darkness and silence crashing down.

Scott Westerfeld's other novels include *The Last Days*, an ALA Best Book for Young Adults and the sequel to *Peeps*; *So Yesterday*, an ALA Best Book for Young Adults; and the Midnighters trilogy. Hard at work on *Leviathan*, the first book in his next series, Scott alternates summers between New York City and Sydney, Australia. Visit him on the Web at www.scottwesterfeld.com.

Lia Kahn was perfect: rich, beautiful, popular.

Until the accident that nearly killed her.

Now she has been downloaded into a new body that only looks human.

Lia will never feel pain again, she will never age, and she can't ever truly die.

But some miracles come at a price. . . .

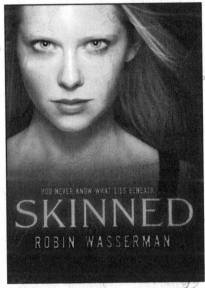

YOU NEVER KNOW WHAT LIES BENEATH.

SKINNED

ROBIN WASSERMAN

THE FIRST BOOK IN A GRIPPING TRILOGY

"A spellbinding story about loss, rebirth,
and finding out who we really are inside.
This intense and moving novel will wind up under your skin."

—SCOTT WESTERFELD

New York Times bestselling author of the Uglies series

From Simon Pulse | Published by Simon & Schuster